"I bought you to be my escort for the reunion," she said in a rush.

He looked genuinely surprised. "Why?"

So many reasons. None of them she wanted to share.

"Guys are probably lined up to take you out."

"Not really." Damn that little glow starting in her belly.

"Molly, I'd have taken you to your reunion even if you hadn't bid on me."

Recently he'd told her she was a knockout. And the geeky adolescent still lurking inside her desperately wanted to believe he meant what he'd said. But she'd believed him once and paid a high price, in self-esteem and trust.

Now she'd made a deal with the devil—or rather, devil-may-care Des. She needed to guard her emotions carefully. To do that, she'd have to keep her mind on the reunion, and only on the reunion.

But just this once, as she closed the door behind her, she'd revel in the intensity burning in his blue eyes as he watched her walk away.

Dear Reader,

Icy winds and fierce snowstorms have nothing on this month's heroines who all seem to have a score to settle. And you know the old line about hell having no fury like a woman scorned—well, grab a hot drink and a comfortable chair and watch what happens when these women dole out their best shots!

Alice Sharpe leads off the month with the final installment in the PERPETUALLY YOURS trilogy. In *A Tail of Love* (#1806), it takes one determined wire fox terrier to convince his stubborn mistress to *stay* with the man she left two years ago. Ever since the big man on campus jilted her in high school, a former plain Jane has wanted revenge…and now his return, her transformation and a bachelor auction provide the perfect opportunity in Teresa Southwick's *In Good Company* (#1807)—the second book in her BUY-A-GUY miniseries. Realizing her groom will always put his work first, a runaway bride heads for the mountains and lands on the doorstep of a man who could give her the storybook ending she craves, in Carol Grace's *Snow White Bride* (#1808), part of her charming FAIRY-TALE BRIDES series. Finally, a computer programmer devises the perfect matchmaking program to exact revenge on her new boss, but she quickly finds that even the best-laid computer program can't account for human attraction, in Judith McWilliams's scintillating romance, *The Matchmaking Machine* (#1809).

Happy reading.

Ann Leslie Tuttle
Associate Senior Editor

Please address questions and book requests to:
Silhouette Reader Service
U.S.: 3010 Walden Ave., P.O. Box 1325, Buffalo, NY 14269
Canadian: P.O. Box 609, Fort Erie, Ont. L2A 5X3

TERESA SOUTHWICK

PRESENTS

In Good Company

Buy
-A-
Guy

SILHOUETTE *Romance*®

Published by Silhouette Books

America's Publisher of Contemporary Romance

SILHOUETTE BOOKS

ISBN 0-373-19807-8

IN GOOD COMPANY

Visit Silhouette Books at www.eHarlequin.com

Printed in U.S.A.

VH
20

Books by Teresa Southwick

Silhouette Romance

Wedding Rings and Baby Things #1209
The Bachelor's Baby #1233
*A Vow, a Ring, a Baby Swing #1349
The Way to a Cowboy's Heart #1383
*And Then He Kissed Me #1405
*With a Little T.L.C. #1421
The Acquired Bride #1474
*Secret Ingredient: Love #1495
*The Last Marchetti Bachelor #1513
**Crazy for Lovin' You #1529
**This Kiss #1541
**If You Don't Know by Now #1560
**What If We Fall in Love? #1572
Sky Full of Promise #1624
†To Catch a Sheik #1674
†To Kiss a Sheik #1686
†To Wed a Sheik #1696
††Baby, Oh Baby #1704
††Flirting with the Boss #1708
††An Heiress on His Doorstep #1712
§That Touch of Pink #1799
§In Good Company #1807

Silhouette Special Edition

The Summer House #1510
"Courting Cassandra"
*Midnight, Moonlight &
Miracles* #1517
It Takes Three #1631
*The Beauty Queen's
Makeover* #1699

Silhouette Books

*The Fortunes of Texas:
Shotgun Vows*

*The Marchetti Family
**Destiny, Texas
†Desert Brides
††If Wishes Were…
§Buy-A-Guy

TERESA SOUTHWICK

lives with her husband in Las Vegas, the city that rein-
vents itself every day. An avid fan of romance novels,
she is delighted to be living out her dream of writing for
Silhouette Books.

Do you need a man?
The 75TH semi-annual
Charity City Buy-A-Guy Auction

This is your chance to find the right one
for that "honey do" list!

Could you use a weekend warrior? Ex-U.S. Army Ranger
Riley Dixon is the guy for you. He's donating a survival
weekend guaranteed to get your heart rate up.

What about that home repair you've been putting off?
Dashing Des O'Donnell, former Charity City High
football hero, now owner and president of his own
construction company, is offering a repair of your choice.

Personal security issues? Defend your honor?
Savvy Sam Brimstone, recently of the LAPD
and a hotshot detective, is your man.

These are just a sampling of the jaw-dropping guys
available to the highest bidder. Ladies, don't miss the
chance to buy a guy—no strings attached.

Cash, Check, Credit and Debit cards gratefully accepted
by the Charity City Philanthropic Foundation.

Chapter One

Charity City, Texas
Mid September, two weeks before the bi-annual
town auction

Desmond O'Donnell was back. Like the Terminator.
Or a bad penny. Or both.

Molly Preston watched him walk past her classroom
window, wishing he looked like a troll. But, where Des
O'Donnell was concerned, her luck had never been that
good. Now was no exception. All she could see was his
profile and that was still to die for.

She was dabbing green paint on construction paper
with one of her kids, when he entered her classroom and
began looking around. She took a good look, too. The

rumor mill had been working overtime since Des had returned to Charity City, and reports of his hunk quotient bordered on the stuff of urban legend. The reports were annoyingly accurate.

Ever since she learned the Charity City Foundation had awarded First Step Preschool the money for a new wing of classrooms and Des had won the contract to build it, she'd known their paths would cross. Again. But he'd picked a bad time to drop in. Not that any time would have been especially good, but it was craft time for her pre-K kids and when paint was involved, it was always uncharted territory. On top of that, a handsome stranger's appearance was like a shot of adrenaline to her four-year-old charges.

They weren't the only ones. Her twenty-five-year-old hormones whipped her heart into a serious palpitation. And her hands were sweating. She was no good around men—never had been, never would be—especially not around one who looked like he should be on the cover of *Carpentry Quarterly*.

Still, she'd been preparing herself to deal with him. But this time she wasn't an overweight, orthodontically challenged, four-eyed high-school girl, easily dazzled by the PHAT—pretty hot and tempting—captain of the football team.

This time, she was a woman, and a professional. More classrooms meant more kids getting a head start on learning—a start that would make them kind, caring and productive members of society.

Seeing Des again was no big deal. Probably he was no longer a jerk. Probably there was a Mrs. Des at home. Besides, Molly was so over him. She was prepared to be polite and helpful because there was no longer any reason to hate his guts.

Brave self-talk, but as she walked over to the man from her past who was standing just inside the classroom door, her tongue felt suddenly three sizes too big for her mouth.

"Hello," she managed to say.

"Hi. I'm Des O'Donnell from O'Donnell Construction."

That sounded an awful lot like an introduction. Their previous acquaintance, such as it was, would suggest dispensing with introductions. She blinked, then stared at him, waiting for some hint of recognition on his part. She saw none.

When she didn't say anything, he continued. "I'll be building the new wing for the preschool and I'm here to look over the construction site."

"I see."

"This classroom will be affected. In the office I was told that this is Polly Preston's room. That would probably make you Miss Preston. May I call you Polly?"

"Sure." Her stomach knotted but her inner smart aleck picked up the slack. "But I can't promise to answer."

"Oh?"

"My name is Molly. Molly Preston."

"Sorry. My mistake."

He didn't look sorry, Molly thought, then reminded herself she didn't need to be snarky because she didn't care. "No problem."

He grinned his charming grin and that *was* a problem. "Nice to meet you, Molly."

Clearly he didn't remember her or her name. She wasn't sure whether or not that was more humiliating than him taking a payoff to date her. After a socially dismal beginning to her freshman year, her father had paid Des to date her and ensure her high-school popularity. Des should have gone into acting. He'd pulled it off without her suspecting a thing. She'd never have known his interest in her was a sham if a disgruntled girlfriend hadn't ratted him out.

Des had used her as a stepping stone to success. He'd got what he wanted, then hadn't had the decency to break it off with her face-to-face. He'd simply stood her up then left for college.

Screw the high road, she decided. His betrayal had unraveled the fabric of her self-esteem. Now he didn't even *remember* her? She would never be grown up enough to not care about that, and she felt justified in her crabbiness.

"Yeah, nice," she lied. "Look, Mr. O'Donnell—"

"Des," he interrupted.

"Des," she repeated, annoyed at how easily his name slipped from her lips. She hoped that only she noticed that her voice had dropped into the seductive range on the single syllable.

Time had been good to Des O'Donnell. He'd always been the stuff of girlish fantasies. Now he was a man, with the filled-out physique to prove it. His chest-and-biceps-hugging navy T-shirt brought out the extraordinary sapphire blue of his eyes. She remembered that his hair had a natural wave when he needed a haircut, which he didn't at the moment. She missed the curl. Once light blond, his hair had changed color over time. Somehow, the darker shade suited him better.

His face had matured, lines fanning out at the corners of his eyes. His square jaw gave him a rugged appearance that was just right on him. And just wrong for her.

The years melted away, turning her back into that insecure, geeky teenager who'd learned that someone like her didn't snag sincere attention from men. Bruce the Bottom-feeder had happened in college. Her mistake had been believing he was the polar opposite of Des. It seemed that every time she went on to a higher level of education, painful personal lessons were involved. Which made her wary of a postgraduate degree.

But she was no longer in high school or college. She was a grown-up responsible for the welfare of the children in her class. It was time to behave that way.

"Look, Des—"

"So I guess we'll be seeing a lot of each other during the construction," he said at the same time.

"It would appear that way."

"Arrangements will have to be made when your classroom is impacted by the construction. I'll need to go over the work schedule with you."

Molly tucked her hands into the pockets of her slacks. "Okay. But it can't be right now."

"Why not?"

"The children are involved in crafts. And that requires my undivided attention."

She glanced over her shoulder and noticed one of the boys painting on the table instead of his paper. Thank goodness for butcher paper and her advance preparation for this very thing. "See what I mean? Now if you'll excuse me—"

"I won't take much of your time."

"Children are schedule-sensitive. The slightest disruption can throw their world into chaos."

"Then why did the office send me over?"

"We have a new receptionist. I'll talk to her."

"It wasn't the receptionist who gave me the green light." He folded his arms over his impressive chest. "I spoke to Mrs. Farris, the director. She said to tell you if you need backup while we discuss business to let her know."

The little table-painter had wandered over beside her. When he slipped his hand into hers, Molly felt the sticky wetness and guessed she now had a green palm.

The boy looked up at the tall visitor. "Hi."

"Hey, buddy," Des replied.

Molly knew if this wasn't nipped in the bud, the rest

of her Picassos-in-training would be joining them, resulting in anarchy. Something any preschool teacher worth her salt would avoid at all cost.

"Trey," she said to the child, "it's craft time. Are you finished with your trees?"

"Yup."

She glanced over to where he'd been sitting and saw his pristine paper with green paint all around it. "Are you sure?" she asked.

Des followed her gaze. "Looks like Trey thinks outside the box."

The four remaining children at the table were getting restless. "Look, Des, this isn't a good time. I have to clean up this group. The rest of my class is outside on the playground with an aide and they're due in any minute for their turn at craft time. I try to stagger it for all my kids so it's a relaxing and creative experience. So, Trey, I want you to go wash your hands."

"But I wanna see what he's gonna do," the boy explained, pointing a green finger at Des. "Do you know Bob the Builder?"

Des squatted, bracing one denim-clad knee on the indoor/outdoor carpet as he rested his tanned forearm on the other. She noticed the way the material pulled snugly at his muscular thigh, then averted her gaze when her pulse jumped.

"Trey, I'm not going to do anything fun," he said, his voice deep, calm and patient. "I'm just going to measure and write stuff down."

The child looked disappointed. "You're not gonna hammer?"

"Not today."

"How come?"

"Because I don't have anything to hammer. I have to order wood and nails and I don't know how much I'll need yet. I'm here to figure that out."

"Oww."

Molly turned at the cry of distress to see a curly-haired brunette rubbing her head.

"What's wrong, Amy?"

"Kyle pulled my hair, Miss Molly," she said, her bottom lip trembling.

"Kyle, remember what I told you about keeping your hands to yourself?"

The towheaded boy nodded. "She started it. She put paint on my new shoe, Miss Molly. My mom said I couldn't even get these new shoes dirty or wet."

"Don't worry. The paint will come off. Did you tell Amy your shoes were new?"

He nodded. "But she painted 'em anyway. She's stupid and I hate—"

Molly held up her finger. The guilty look on Kyle's face told her he'd remembered too late her pet peeve—calling someone names. She'd been on the receiving end of enough hurtful taunts and wouldn't permit name-calling in her classroom. Children weren't too young to learn good manners and it was her goal to plant the seeds of kindness in as many of them as she could. But she tried to be fair when dispensing consequences.

She walked over to the pint-size squabblers. "Amy," she said, squatting at the low table between the two children. She glanced at the black streak on the boy's formerly snow-white sneaker. "Did you put paint on Kyle's shoe?"

"Yes, but—"

Molly held up her hand. "No excuses. Please put down your paintbrush." The little girl did as she was told. "Now, tell Kyle you're sorry for what you did."

"Sorry," she mumbled.

Molly looked at the boy. "Kyle, you need to say you're sorry for pulling Amy's hair and calling her names."

His stubborn expression clearly said he'd been wronged and shouldn't have to apologize. But Molly sternly met his gaze without flinching. Every transgression required an apology even if hostilities hadn't been initiated by the apologizer. Good thing she hadn't held her breath waiting for Des to apologize for making a fool of her.

Finally Kyle rubbed a finger beneath his nose and said, "Sorry, Amy."

"Good," Molly said, nodding with satisfaction. "Now I want everyone to come with me to the sink and we'll wash our hands."

"But Trey is talkin' to the man," Kyle said, pointing. "Why can't we?"

"Because after painting we have to make sure our

hands are clean before we do anything else. And Trey is going to wash up, too."

Molly walked her charges to the tot-size sinks and got them started. When they were finished, she lined them up by the door to the playground. "I'll be right back."

She walked to where man and boy were still talking.

"The boards are cut to the right length, then I'm going to put them together with nails," Des was saying.

"Can I watch?" Trey asked.

"Sure."

"He said I could watch," Trey told her excitedly.

"I heard." Molly reined in her irritation. She needed a word—or twenty—with this man. Preferably when no children were present and she could freely speak her mind.

"Can I help?" the boy eagerly asked.

"I don't see why not." Des smiled at the child.

"Trey, it's time to wash your hands. Then line up with the others." Molly touched his shoulder and turned him, gently nudging him in the direction of the sinks. He reluctantly went, glancing over his shoulder several times. When the boy was on task, she looked at Des. "May I speak to you in the time-out room?"

He straightened to his full six-foot-plus height. His eyebrows, a shade darker than his hair, rose along with the corners of his mouth. Something amused him. No doubt her. It seemed she was destined to be his comic relief.

"This sounds serious. Am I in trouble?"

Only if breaking hearts was a hanging offense. Hers had been a casualty. But she wouldn't stand by and see him play fast and loose with a child's emotions.

"Let's not disrupt the children further. We can discuss it in there." She indicated the small storage area off her classroom with windows that gave her a view of her charges. When they entered the room, she turned quickly, colliding with the man who followed her. He was all lean muscle, wiry strength and warm male flesh. It was like walking into a brick wall, and just as hard on her system.

"Sorry," she mumbled, quickly stepping back.

"Why? You didn't call me stupid." So he'd heard her with the children. Apparently the man could multi-task. He pointed at the glass and said, "Is this like the two-way mirrors the police use? We can see them, but they can't see us?"

"No, actually. They can see us."

He rested his hands on narrow hips. What was it about a man in jeans that spelled danger for female hearts? Before going any further with that thought, she stopped herself. She was angry with him, which should leave no room for thoughts like that.

"Wait here. The other kids are coming inside and I need to have my aide hold down the fort for a few minutes."

Des watched through the glass as Molly Preston walked across her classroom to talk to a tall, jean-clad woman with a whistle around her neck. He frowned, wondering what Miss Molly's problem was. He hoped she wasn't the type who got her panties in a twist over the small stuff.

And speaking of panties, he had a feeling Miss Molly filled hers out in the nicest possible way. She was quite a package. It was the first thing he'd noticed when he walked into her classroom. She was petite, pretty and pleasingly proportioned in all the right places. Then there were the thick auburn curls teasing her shoulders. He had the most absurd urge to run his fingers through her hair to see if it was as silky and soft as it looked. And familiar. Why was that?

Actually, their paths had probably crossed. He'd grown up in this town but couldn't wait to leave. His father's death had brought him back to salvage the company his grandfather had started. Des had pumped a lot of his own money into the failing construction business, so he had a lot riding on the success of the preschool project. The profit margin was real narrow, but profit wasn't his goal. This was simply a stepping stone to the real prize—a contract with Richmond Homes for the new development south of Charity City.

He was in negotiations right now with Carter Richmond who'd said in no uncertain terms he'd be watching Des's work. In a town the size of Charity City, one black mark on a man's reputation could be his loss and a competitor's gain. Des knew that if he was to keep his business afloat, losing contracts wasn't an option. He needed to build the wing of classrooms on time, within budget, and it had to be the best work he'd ever done. Besides that, a good businessman never underestimated the value of word of mouth in a town the size of Charity City. For all of the above, he needed Miss Molly's cooperation.

When she walked back into the interrogation room, he said, "So, what did you want to talk to me about?"

"So many things, so little time." Her gaze narrowed.

This was not exactly the most convenient moment to notice what interesting things irritation did to her green eyes.

"What's on your mind?" he prompted. If this was going to go smoothly, they needed to get all their cards on the table.

"For starters, I have a problem with you promising Trey that he could help you."

Des shrugged. "He seemed interested. A boy can't start too young. My grandfather started teaching me to work with wood when I was about Trey's age."

"Let's forget the liability issue for now. Let's go straight to the part where Trey comes from a single-parent home—his mother being the only parent there. His dad is out of the picture."

Des wondered how that was a bad thing. If he had a nickel for every time he'd wished he didn't have a father, money would never have been an issue. "Lack of male influence is all the more reason to let him help me."

Molly's frown deepened. "So you pay attention to a lonely little boy. What happens to him when you walk out of his life? And you will."

Where did she get off judging him? They'd just met. He stared down at her. "Even if that's true, and you can't know it is, isn't some positive male influence even for a short time better than none at all?"

Her full mouth tightened for a moment. "From personal experience, I'd have to say no."

"Oo-kay." He blew out a long breath.

Now what? The school director had made it clear that because her classroom was involved in the renovation, he had to coordinate schedules with this teacher. First, he had to find out what was bugging her, then figure out how to fix it.

"Look, Molly, like you said, I've come at a bad time. Maybe it would be best to discuss this when you're not so busy with kids."

"You're right. This isn't a good time."

Stubborn as a mule. But it looked good on her, in spite of her attitude from hell. It made him want to lean over and touch his mouth to hers—to shock the stubborn right out of her.

"Okay. Not a good time. We finally agree on something." He rubbed his hands together. "How about this? I'll take you out for dinner and we can—"

She held up her hand. "No way."

He wanted to ask why not, but decided not to go

there. Compromise and negotiation. "Then how about a drink after work?"

"I don't think so. Any discussion would be best conducted here on school grounds."

He recognized a shutdown when he saw it, and he would admit to some ego. Women had always paid attention to him, which had made for a bitter lesson when he'd learned that attention and respect for who he really was were two very different things. It was a mistake he wouldn't repeat. But that was personal. This was business; he was good at business. He knew when someone was giving him the business. The question was…why? Molly Preston was a puzzle he couldn't wrap his mind around. But she was about to learn he'd invented the word *stubborn*.

He nodded. "When would be a good time to talk?"

Her look said when the devil ice-skated in hell, but she answered, "The children are all supposed to be picked up by six o'clock."

"Then I'll see you at six sharp."

She opened her mouth to say something but he moved toward the door, refusing to give her a chance to stonewall him. Right now he needed to have a word with the preschool director. Maybe Mrs. Farris could shed some light on the mystifying Molly Preston.

After leaving her classroom, he crossed the courtyard and entered the administration building where Molly's boss happened to be standing by the desk in the reception area. She was blond, attractive, probably in her early to mid-fifties, and trim.

He stopped in front of her. "Hi."

She smiled. "You're already finished? Obviously you and Molly work well together."

"Actually, I wanted to talk to you about that."

The woman frowned. "Uh-oh. No one wants to talk if everything's okay."

"Yeah. You got that right."

"There was a problem with Molly?"

He nodded. "Apparently I rub her the wrong way."

"I'm stunned. She's not your typical stubborn redhead. I've never known her to be anything but easygoing and mellow. Molly gets along with everyone."

"Then apparently I'm her first," he said ruefully. "I tried to talk to her about the building schedule, I think I got on her bad side. Somehow."

Mrs. Farris looked surprised. "I don't get it. If anyone would understand the importance of building schedules, it's Molly."

"Why's that?"

"Molly's father is a home builder. You may have heard of him. Carter Richmond, of Richmond Homes."

"But I thought her last name was Preston?"

"That's her married name."

Des felt as if he'd just been hit by a big steel wrecking ball. Her maiden name gave him the missing piece of the puzzle and the picture wasn't pretty.

He was the guy who'd done her wrong.

Chapter Two

Standing across the courtyard, Des watched Molly safely hand off the last of her kids to an authorized adult. He'd been waiting there for half an hour. Heaven forbid he was thirty seconds late; she'd be so out of there to avoid him. Which wasn't a disaster, really. It would simply delay the inevitable. Because he *would* talk to her. When he did, he would up the wattage on his charm. It had only failed him once, a personal failure he didn't intend to repeat. Dealing with Molly was business, and from now on he was all business, all the time.

Unfortunately, he had his work cut out for him with Molly. He wasn't proud of how he'd broken things off with her in high school, but that wasn't the worst. Had she told her father she'd seen him with another girl, prompting the man to tell her everything? It was supposed to be their secret, part of the agreement he'd made with Carter Richmond. But Des had no idea how low the man could stoop.

Clearly Molly hadn't forgiven him for what she did know. If, by some miracle, she was in the dark about the rest, he'd be an idiot to bring it up. Right now he was looking at major damage control, which would no doubt include a long-overdue apology. He needed Molly on his side.

When she started back into her classroom, he walked quickly across the courtyard. "Wait, Molly."

Her spine went as straight as a two-by-four just before she turned to face him. "You're back."

"I said I'd be here at six sharp," he answered, noting the way the pulse in her neck fluttered like crazy.

"So you did." Her tone was as starchy as her body.

It didn't take a mental giant to read between the lines and figure out she hadn't expected him to keep his word. Why should she after what he'd done? Or maybe she'd simply been hoping he'd give up and go away. If so, she was about to find out how wrong she was. She might seem stiff and uncooperative on the outside, but her pounding pulse told him that Miss Molly Preston was as nervous as a roofer with vertigo.

Charm don't fail me now, he thought. "Look, Molly, I need to apologize to you."

"Oh?" One auburn eyebrow rose.

"I was a jerk—"

"Yes, you were," she interrupted. "You need to think before promising something to a child."

He shook his head. "I meant when we were in high school."

"So you finally figured out who I am," she said, hostility lacing her words.

"I remembered you." He recognized her Yeah-right expression and added, "After Mrs. Farris told me Preston is your married name."

"Hmm."

"I treated you badly—"

"It's water over the bridge. Or under the dam. Or whatever. It was a long time ago," she said stiffly.

"It was," he agreed. "I was hoping we could put it behind us and start again." Des studied her, the slight pucker in the otherwise smooth skin of her forehead.

She met his gaze directly and her green eyes darkened. "I don't think so."

It had been too much to hope that she didn't know he'd made a deal with her father to pay attention to her. It would take several Dr. Phils to sort out the psychological fallout from that. All things considered, Des didn't blame her for not making this easy, but the Molly he'd known years ago probably would have. When he'd started paying attention to her, he'd been playing a part, but her sweetness and sassy sense of humor had won him over. He'd liked her a lot. Oddly, he liked this tougher Molly, too.

"It was a long time ago but obviously you're still upset."

"About the past?" She folded her arms over her chest as she leaned against the doorjamb.

"Yeah. The part where I was young and stupid." He braced himself for her to blast him about pretending feelings for her.

"How innocuous that sounds. Why should it still bother me that you stood me up? Or maybe you're referring to the fact that I saw you kissing Kelli Arnold at the movie you were supposed to take me to."

"I handled it badly. I was going away to college and figured a quick break was better. Like pulling off a bandage. It hurts for a second, then it's over."

"You can't be serious."

"Why not?"

"Young and stupid is no excuse for your behavior," she said.

"I agree. But with age comes wisdom and…" He flashed his trademark grin, the one women seemed to respond to. "And, hopefully, redemption."

Her gaze narrowed on him. "You really think I'm upset about what happened in high school?"

Correction: most women. He didn't see any let up in the mad Molly had going on. The good news was, she didn't seem to know her father had bribed him to date her. If she did, nothing would have stopped her from listing it in her grievances against him. Now that he thought about it, why would Carter Richmond admit to something so slimy and underhanded? That secret was safe.

"You have every right to be upset."

She shook her head as if he were the dumbest person on the planet. "Oh, please."

Okay. Now he was confused. If she wasn't in a snit about his high school transgressions, what was her problem? Maybe it was time to admit defeat and throw himself on her mercy. "Okay, then I give up. What's bugging you?"

"I can't believe you have to ask." She rolled her eyes. "May I call you Polly?"

Suddenly the "aha" light went on. This was easy. Time to turn up the amps on his charm. But as he looked into her big green eyes and that flawless face, he found he didn't need charm. All he needed was the truth.

"You're ticked off because I didn't recognize you."

"Bingo."

"It was an honest mistake. And there's a really good reason. You've changed, Molly."

"Not that much."

"Yeah, that much. And more. You've lost your baby fat."

"How diplomatic of you to phrase it that way. No more mega-Molly?"

"I never called you that."

"To my face," she challenged.

"Or behind your back. And there's something else. Your glasses are gone. No offense, Molly, you're a knockout now. But you have to admit, in high school you wouldn't have won any beauty contests."

Her gaze narrowed. "Then why did you hang out with me?"

Uh-oh. Now he was on thin ice. He couldn't tell her the truth. What she had on him was bad enough and he hoped she'd never find out the rest—for her sake, and because he wasn't the same person he'd been back then, someone desperate for a way out of Charity City.

And that was when it hit him. The woman he'd fallen in love with, the one he'd thought loved him back, was just as shallow as the person he used to be. Wasn't that just a healthy dose of poetic justice! But he couldn't tell Molly any of that.

Once again, honesty was the best policy. "I hung out with you because you were smart and funny. And sweet." It hadn't started out that way, but eventually it had become the truth.

"Ah, the old you-have-a-great-personality defense."

"It's true. At least, it was then. I'm not so sure now."

She pushed off the doorjamb and looked at him skeptically. "You're telling me that Des O'Donnell, big man on campus who could have had any girl he wanted, hung out with me because he liked me?"

"In a nutshell? Yeah," he said.

"I find that hard to believe. Teenage boys are notoriously shallow. You're no longer a teenage boy," she said, swallowing as her gaze dropped to the center of his chest. "But I suspect you haven't changed much."

"We haven't seen each other in years. You know nothing about the person I am now. Whatever happened to innocent until proven guilty?" he asked, resting his hands on his hips.

"Leopards don't change their spots."

"That's not true." He thought about his words and said, "Technically it's true. But your implication that I couldn't have changed is wrong."

"Depends on whose truth you're talking about. Mine is that you're the same self-centered, egotistical person you were in high school."

"And you're not willing to give me the benefit of the doubt?"

"I don't think so. You've already revealed your character to me. Going back for seconds isn't especially bright. Fool me once, shame on you. Fool me twice, shame on me."

"Speaking of character, I'm not in the habit of inviting married women to dinner. I said that before I found out you're not single."

"I'm divorced," she clarified.

Now why in the world should that information make him happy? Clearly she was hostile toward him and at the very least reluctant to cut him any slack. But the fact was, he was glad she wasn't married. "Okay. Then will you reconsider having dinner with me tonight?"

"No. Now if you'll excuse me, Des, I've got things to do." She started to close the door.

He put his palm against it, refusing to let her dismiss

him. He knew she wasn't inclined to let bygones be bygones. He couldn't blame her. Didn't he feel the same about not repeating his own mistake? But he had a job to do and he intended to get it done. For that, he needed her cooperation. And he fully intended to get it.

"Look, Molly, I'm going to put all my cards on the table."

"That would be a first," she muttered.

"Obviously you don't think very much of me. And believe it or not, I can't say I blame you. But here's the thing. I'm going to be doing the new preschool wing. Whether you approve or not."

"It's a pity no one asked for my opinion." She clapped a hand over her mouth. "I can't believe I said that. Isn't bringing out the worst in me enough reason for you to give up?"

"No. You don't have to agree with the decision, but, like it or not, we're going to have to work together. It would be more pleasant and certainly far more efficient if we could do that as friends."

"Friends is asking too much." She sighed. "But I'm committed to this school. And the expansion is impor-tant. So, for the sake of that, I agree that an armed truce is necessary in achieving the goal that we both want."

Des nodded. "I'm glad there's something we agree on." Instinct told him to press his advantage. "To that end, we need to discuss the project and how it will affect your classroom."

"All right." She caught her top lip between her teeth

as she thought for a moment. "Come by tomorrow and we can talk about it."

"Third time's the charm. What about dinner? It would give us an opportunity to go over things without interruption. That's hard to do with the kids around."

"Apparently I haven't made myself clear." She settled her hand on her hip and met his gaze. "I love my job. And I'm devoted to the children in my care."

"I can see that."

"I would do anything to improve this facility and give even more children an opportunity for a positive beginning to their education."

"Great. I know this restaurant in town—"

She held up her hand. "Dinner is not part of the armed truce. Whatever we need to talk about can be discussed on school grounds."

"I'm sorry you feel that way."

Des found he truly meant that. The prospect of getting to know the grown-up Molly was intriguing because she was more than just a pretty face. She was intelligent, witty and a complicated woman. He had a fleeting regret that he'd probably destroyed any chance with her.

She started to close the door again. "So, if you'll excuse me, I have things to do to get ready for tomorrow."

"Okay. I'll see you then."

He backed up and she shut the door in his face. Out in the cold. And dark. And Des didn't much like it. Since when had he become the kind of guy who rolled

over and played dead when things didn't go his way?
He wasn't his father. Failure wasn't an option. He would
find a way to get on Miss Molly's good side.

On her way home Molly stopped at the supermarket
next door to her apartment complex. When the automatic doors whispered open, she grabbed a basket and
headed for the pasta aisle to pick up a whole-wheat
rigatoni and a jar of marinara sauce.

The fact that she had nothing at home for dinner
hadn't even tempted her to accept Des's invitation.
What *had* tempted her was his devil-may-care grin and
in-your-face sex appeal. She'd taken cover behind her
anger and effectively quelled any possible leftover
weakness from her own young-and-stupid days. So why
didn't she feel more empowered about turning him
down? Probably she needed her head examined.

As she walked toward the produce aisle, an image
of Des popped into her head. He'd seemed surprised
by her refusal to have dinner with him, which convinced her he didn't know she knew about the bribe
from her father. If she'd told him she knew everything,
that would have certainly cleared up his confusion. But
bringing up the past would only resurrect her humiliation. Who wanted to remember being such a
disappointment to Daddy that he'd felt he had to buy
her popularity? Where was the win in reminding Des
about that?

No, the past was the past. But avoiding Des in the

present was impossible because of the preschool expansion. She simply had to suck it up and tough it out. Then go on with her life as if Des had never come back into it.

She rounded the corner and stopped short. Speak of the devil. Of all the grocery stores in all the world, Des had to show up in hers. Maybe she could back away before he saw her. But he picked that moment to look up from the artfully arranged rows of greens and do a double take, followed by his take-no-prisoners grin. Busted. That made escape with dignity impossible.

When he started toward her, she knew it was too much to hope that he would simply let her nod politely and continue on her merry way.

He stopped in front of her. "Hello again."

"Hi." She tucked her hair behind her ear. "What are you doing here?"

Besides raising her temperature, she thought. It was hot. Normally she froze in the market. But tonight she was warm all over and wondered why the iceberg lettuce wasn't wilting.

"I'm here to buy groceries."

Well, of course he was. Stupid question. Then another thought popped into her mind.

"Why this store?" she asked suspiciously.

One corner of his mouth quirked up. "You mean, am I following you?"

If only, she thought, followed quickly by God forbid.

She didn't want him following her; she wanted nothing to do with him.

"Of course not. I just wondered… This is my regular store. I simply meant—" She sighed and let the unfinished thought hang there.

"As a matter of fact, this is the store closest to my apartment," he said.

"You don't mean the ones on Cooper Street?"

"The very ones," he confirmed.

Her heart sank, hit bottom, then bounced into her throat. That was where her apartment was. Why hadn't she known he was living there? Surely her overactive heat sensors would have picked up his presence. On the other hand, it was a very large complex.

"Your regular store," he repeated. "Do you live nearby, too?"

"Actually in the same complex on Cooper. That would make us neighbors," she finished lamely. "So you're here for groceries."

A smile teased the corners of his mouth. "Remind me to watch out for you. Mind like a steel trap."

"Oh, knock it off," she said, annoyed with herself for stating the obvious. Again. At the same time she wanted to laugh.

"Okay. Yes, I was forced to stop for food because someone refused my dinner invitation."

"No," she answered in mock astonishment. "Who could possibly resist the legendary O'Donnell charm?"

"You'd be surprised." Something like anger flashed

in his eyes, then almost as quickly disappeared. He grinned, but the effort showed. "Actually, there's this redhead in town who finds me completely resistible."

"Oh?" Her cheeks warmed.

"Yes." He made a great show of studying the items in her basket. "Looks like Italian night at your house."

She shrugged. "It's easy."

"Not as easy as a restaurant," he pointed out.

"True. But much less complicated."

"I'm not complicated. I'm the essence of simplicity. In fact, since we're neighbors, it would be simple for me to drop by and see if you cook as well as you mold the minds of Charity City youth."

Simple for him, maybe. Not for her. Sitting across from him at a restaurant would have been high enough on the intimacy scale. But sitting across from him in her apartment would send intimacy into the danger zone. She'd already spent time in that zone. It hadn't worked for her then, and she had no reason to think anything had changed. And, for crying out loud, hadn't they already gone through this?

"Tonight's not good," she hedged.

"Are you cooking for someone else?"

"No," she said quickly, then kicked herself. That would have been a good out, but she'd missed it. What was wrong with her? He'd told her she was a knock-out. Although her geeky, self-conscious, socially challenged inner child didn't believe him. What was it about this man that scrambled her thought processes?

"So you're doing spaghetti solo because it's not a good night?" He stuck a hand in the pocket of his battered brown leather jacket.

"Look, I already told you that—"

"We talk only on school grounds," he finished. "Don't look now, but we're in the grocery store. And we're talking."

How was she going to get through to him? Scrambled thought processes would be a step up from what her mind was doing. Meltdown would be more accurate. Especially when one took into account the radioactive heat generated by close proximity to Des's special brand of animal magnetism. But now she had to come up with an excuse to brush him off. And being abrasive didn't come naturally to her. The tough facade she was putting on wouldn't hold up much longer because she felt certain even a man like Des had feelings to hurt. So she was reluctant to be so direct again. That was why she said the first thing that came to mind.

"Dinner isn't a good idea in a small town like this."

"You mean folks in small towns don't eat an evening meal?" he asked, feigning a completely serious expression.

The corners of her mouth twitched, but she refused to be amused. From letting him amuse her it was a hop, skip and jump to rekindling her crush. And that wasn't funny.

"It's like this, Des. I'm a teacher—"

"Teachers don't eat?"

"Yes, of course we do. But I'm not comfortable sharing dinner in my apartment with a man. It's a small town."

"So you said."

"I'm a teacher," she said again.

"And a fine one, too. I could tell."

"It's a recipe for scandal. Everyone talks. The good, bad and ugly spreads like wildfire. I just don't think I want to go there."

"Hmm. Oddly enough, that sounds pretty good to me after the big city where everyone is a stranger and no one gives a damn what anyone else does."

The anger flared in his eyes again and Molly wondered about it. What had happened to Des since he'd left town all those years ago? She knew he'd gone to college, but that was all. Abruptly, she put the lid on those thoughts. This was bad. Curiosity about his life was worse than bad. It was downright dangerous.

"I've got to go," she said.

Before he could respond, she turned and headed for the cash register to pay for her pathetic dinner. So what if she hadn't picked up salad fixings? Lack of roughage wasn't the end of the world, but continued closeness to Des could be. So what if he thought her social skills as backward as they'd been all those years ago? She couldn't afford to care what he thought.

Curiosity about him meant that her interest was escalating. She had to nip that in the bud, then ideally work to become indifferent. Soon, she vowed, she would feel nothing for Desmond O'Donnell. No shortness of breath. No heart palpitations. Come to think of it, her symptoms resembled a heart attack—which was exactly what she was trying to avoid. At all costs, she needed to protect her heart.

When she felt nothing for him, she would be home free. And speaking of home, this town was hers. He'd left, but she'd made her life here.

She wouldn't let him waltz in and mess that up. Again.

Chapter Three

"It shouldn't be this hard to get a man."

"Maybe not for you. But the rest of us aren't so lucky." Molly looked at her beautiful blond friend and sighed.

Charity had a look that shifted effortlessly from girl-next-door cute to lingerie-model sexy. She was a Wentworth, a descendant of the town's founding family. She was a Paris-trained chef, although if she never worked a day in her life, her rich-and-famous lifestyle wouldn't suffer. Unlike Molly, who wouldn't take a dime from her dad, Charity had a good relationship with her father.

Charity was five years older so they hadn't known each other in high school and when Molly joined the Charity City Foundation auction committee, she'd expected a snooty and condescending Charity Wentworth. Nothing could be further from the truth. In short, Charity was practically perfect. Except for the part where as chairwoman of the committee she had put Molly in charge of finding men willing to donate their time for auction.

With just under two weeks until the auction, Charity had called this strategic planning session at Molly's antique oak dining-room table. Charity was meeting with volunteers in charge of different subcommittees to make sure the event came off without a hitch. She also chaired the foundation that distributed grants.

"We need more men," Charity reminded her. "This is the seventy-fifth anniversary of the very first auction, which started during the Depression."

"Thanks for the history lesson."

"*I'll* be history if we bomb. The folks are putting the pressure on Jack and me to raise more money than ever before. We need volunteers, and lots of them. If they fetch a pretty penny, so much the better."

"Well, Houston, you've got a serious problem," Molly said. "I'm no good with men. Never was, never will be."

"You don't have to be good with them. You just have to get them to give up some time. Convince them that volunteering for Buy-a-Guy is character-building and good for the soul."

"Volunteering," Molly said, shaking her head. "That's how it starts. All I wanted to do was give a little back to the town. Maybe start a recycling program.

Plant a tree. Clean up graffiti. But this is what happens when you miss a planning meeting. Someone puts you in charge of what no one else wants to do."

Charity grinned. "There are worse things than being in charge of men."

Yeah, Molly thought. *Not* being in charge. Of one man. The one she couldn't seem to get off her mind. One Desmond O'Donnell.

"I'm just not the sort of woman who inspires men to get in touch with their inner nobility. No man has ever thrown his cloak over a puddle so I didn't soil my dainty feet. Mostly they just dump on me. Getting a man to line up and wait for orders is your sphere of expertise, Charity. Not mine."

Long blond hair swung from side to side as the other woman shook her head. "If only that were true. But I've had my share of unfortunate experiences. Very, very public experiences. I have orders from my father to keep a low profile."

"Good luck. The only way to accomplish that is to go out in public with a bag over your head."

Charity laughed, then turned serious. "I know male recruitment's a lousy job, Mol. But someone has to do it."

"If I'd known this was going to happen," Molly grumbled, "I'd have found another outlet for my philanthropic pursuits."

"Look, you can continue to whine. Or we can work together to get the job done. My brother doesn't think

I'm up to the challenge and I'm determined to make Black Jack Wentworth eat his words."

"Black Jack?" Molly's eyes widened. "Your brother sounds intriguing."

"He has a past."

"Don't we all." Reluctant to talk about her own, Molly didn't press her friend about Jack.

Charity met her gaze. "Seriously, Mol, this is a big one. Think about it. For seventy-five years, Charity City folks have put their money where their mouths are. The funding is used for the women's shelter, scholarships and start-up capital for new businesses. Where's your civic pride? We need to pool our resources and make this the best event ever."

"Okay. You're right." Molly sighed dramatically. "Besides, whining isn't working. I might as well just suck it up and get on board."

"That's the spirit. And what we need is strategy. It's always harder to get the guys to step up. And that has nothing to do with you or your way with men. I think it's more about testosterone or something." Charity tapped her lip. "Speaking of which, I did have an idea."

"You're going to sprinkle testosterone in the iced tea of every unsuspecting man in town?"

"No way. But there's a lovely little thing called community service. I'll talk to Judge Gibson and see what he can do to help us."

"You're going to recruit convicted felons? How

much do you suppose ex-cons would fetch at auction?" Molly asked wryly.

"First of all, they wouldn't be ex-cons because they haven't been sent up the river. I'm thinking more the slap-on-the-wrist-because-they-had-a-little-too-much-fun sort. Second, it could be profitable. Escaped prisoner and the warden's wife can be a very powerful fantasy."

Molly shook her head. "You know as well as I do that the auction rules prohibit that sort of hanky-panky."

"Yeah." Charity sighed. "More's the pity. But speaking of rules—" she snapped her fingers "—what about Des O'Donnell? He got the preschool expansion project. The auction rules state that anyone who profits from foundation funds has to give back by donating their time."

"Yeah. Des." Molly couldn't believe she hadn't thought of that herself. He was duty-bound to participate. "He's already started working on the new wing."

"Then you won't have to go far to talk to him."

Talking to him was the problem. She was moving heaven and earth to avoid him. Ever since running into him at the grocery store, she'd been peeking around corners and sneaking to her car so she wouldn't encounter him on apartment turf. Her lease was up in a couple months, and she planned to look for another place to live. But that didn't solve her current problem. She needed to figure out a way to convince Charity to approach Des herself. Before she could, there was a knock on her door.

"Are you expecting anyone?"

Molly shook her head. "Probably someone selling magazines."

But when she opened the door, Des was standing there. So much for moving heaven and earth. Whatever he was selling, she had no intention of buying. Besides, she'd been just this side of rude the last time she spoke to him in the grocery store. Why in the world would he show up for more?

"Hi," he said, smiling as if nothing had happened. As if women abruptly turned their backs on him every day. And there was no way that happened. Not to Des.

"Hi. What do you want?"

His gaze slid past her to the dining-room table. "Sorry. Didn't know you were busy."

"Well, I am." He was on the doorstep, not inside. She embraced the technicality as a reason *not* to introduce him to Charity. Then she noticed the empty container in his hand. "Did you need something?"

"Coffee. I forgot to buy it at the store the other night. And it's your fault."

"Mine?" she said, pressing a hand to her chest. Darn her heart was beating fast.

"You distracted me. The least you could do is loan me some."

"Molly," Charity said from behind her, "why don't you invite the poor man in?"

Now she was stuck. If she sent him packing, she'd feel like the wicked witch of the Midwest. She stepped aside. "Come in."

He entered, then glanced around. "This is nice. It's different from mine. One bedroom or two?"

"Two. Down there," she said, still avoiding introductions as she pointed past the kitchen island to the long hall. It led to a master bedroom with a walk-in closet and a bath. The room beyond that she used as an office.

Still looking around, he said, "I like what you've done with the place."

"Thanks."

Molly liked it, too. An overstuffed sofa in moss-colored chenille sat across from her entertainment center. Beside the sofa, a door led outside to a small balcony where she'd put a cute white wrought-iron table and two chairs. The interior was ultra-homey, with its knickknacks and artwork on the walls. Golly, she was going to hate to move.

With his index finger, Des nudged aside the lace curtain covering her big picture window and glanced outside. "Nice view. I have a completely unobstructed view of the parking lot."

"Hello? Molly? I'm here." Charity stood and walked over to them. "Hi, Des. Charity Wentworth. Remember me?"

Why hadn't Molly thought of that? Charity had graduated a year before Des and was out of high school before Molly started. But Charity and Des would probably have known each other.

"Sure I remember you. How've you been?" he asked, giving Charity a quick, friendly hug.

"Fine."

Molly watched the two of them, bracing herself for Des to go gaga over her gorgeous friend. Men did that to Charity all the time. And Molly had to admit it would bother her to see Des dote on Charity. Was she so pathetic? She didn't want him, but she didn't want anyone else to have him? Oddly enough, his pleasant look never even inched into gaga territory.

Charity's did, though. She blatantly scrutinized him. "Molly and I were just talking about you."

"Oh?"

Molly's cheeks heated when he met her gaze. "Yes. I mentioned you've started working on the preschool project."

"Yeah. I'm grateful to the school for awarding me the contract."

Charity's blue eyes narrowed as she fixed her gaze on Molly. "We were also talking about how hard it is to find a man and—voilà—one shows up on Molly's doorstep."

"Was there a specific reason you need a man?" he asked, one corner of his mouth curving up.

"For the auction," Molly answered. "We need as many men as we can get."

"Yes," Charity chimed in. "And I believe we have *you* on a technicality."

"I'd be happy to donate my time," he said, getting their drift right away.

Molly was surprised he agreed so readily. She figured he'd find some way to slide out of the technicality part. If there wasn't something in it for him, she felt certain he wasn't the sort to help out.

"Wonderful," Charity said. "To keep the foundation's assistance programs funded, we need help from those who have benefited from the endowment. I appreciate your willingness to get involved."

"It's the least I can do," he agreed. "And I'll recruit my construction crew to volunteer."

"Can you do that?" Molly asked.

"I'm the boss."

Charity hugged him. "That would be awesome. We have a Web site where we post information about our volunteers, the amount of time and any skills they're donating. That way people can decide ahead of time who they want to bid on. I'm going to guess you and the crew build stuff."

"Good guess. I'll get back to you on time commitments for myself and the other guys."

"Good enough," Charity said, nodding.

"Now, Molly, if you could help me out with that sugar, I'll get out of here so the two of you can get back to the business of plotting against the unsuspecting male population of Charity City."

"I thought you wanted coffee," Molly said as she took the container he held out.

"So I did," he said sheepishly.

Molly turned to open her pantry but hadn't missed the gleam in Charity's eyes as she took her seat at the table. After grabbing the large red economy can of coffee, Molly filled Des's plastic container, then handed it back to him. "There."

"Much obliged." He walked to the door. "It was nice to see you again, Charity."

"Same here."

He met Molly's gaze. "See you tomorrow."

Molly nodded, then shut the door after him. Leaning against it, she let out a long breath. When she'd pulled herself together, she walked back to join Charity at the table. "Now, where were we?"

Charity shrugged. "Gosh, I don't know, Mol. Maybe we should start with what's the story with you and Des?"

"What makes you think there's a story?" she hedged.

"He works where you do and you didn't recruit him for the auction when he should have been first on your list. What's up with that?"

"I told you I was no good with men," she defended.

"That's not what I just saw."

"It's not what you think. And I'd rather not dredge up the past."

"So you guys have a past? How come I don't remember?"

Molly so didn't want to talk about this. "I couldn't say. But it was ugly and painful. High-school stuff. If you don't mind, I don't want to talk about it."

"Okay." Her friend looked thoughtful. "Speaking of high school, you got all the information about the reunion festivities coming up?"

"I did."

"You going?"

Molly folded her arms on the table. "Yes."

"You don't exactly look like you're doing the dance of joy at the prospect."

"I'd rather have LASIK surgery without tranquilizers than socialize with the girls who made my high-school years a living hell."

"Then why go?" Charity asked.

"Because my favorite teacher is retiring and there's a special reception. If not for her, I wouldn't have a job I love. The least I can do is show up in her honor."

Charity looked at the door where Des had stood moments before. "I remember now that he was the 'it,' guy in high school. And he's still got 'it.' Seems to me if you had an escort with just the right amount of 'it', the reunion wouldn't be so bad. In fact, don't get mad, get even with those girls who made your life a living hell."

Molly was relieved that Charity only seemed to remember Des's 'it' factor and not her own scandalous history with him. "If by the right escort you mean Des, forget it. No way he'd go with me, even if I wanted him to."

"Come on, Molly. You don't really think he dropped by to borrow coffee, do you?"

"Sure. What other reason would there be?"

"First of all, he couldn't keep his story straight. Second, there's a Starbucks on every corner. He wasn't fooling anyone—except maybe you—with that phony excuse. He came to see you, Mol."

Okay, so he'd come up with an excuse to stop by, but it wasn't about an attraction to her. More likely Des had some ulterior motive. He was the one who'd taught her that women like her didn't inspire gaga behavior in men. Des had shown her that everything he did was calculated.

But two could calculate. And Charity just might have suggested a way to support the auction, survive the reunion, and get a little satisfaction while she was at it.

Des hadn't been to the Charity City Community Center since he was about twelve, when he used to play pickup basketball to escape his father's drunken binges. Tonight, auction night, instead of kids letting off steam, rows of chairs were filled with folks eager to do their part in funding the town's charitable foundation. Some people, like Molly, did more than their part to make sure the worthwhile cause continued.

From his position at the rear of the center, just inside the doorway, he had no trouble spotting her red hair, bright as a beacon on a stormy night, in the third row from the stage. She was sitting between a brunette with sun-streaked highlights and an older couple. So far none of them had bought a guy. But the night wasn't over. Right now there was a break in the auction action.

"Hello again."

Des glanced to his right and recognized Charity

Wentworth. "Hi. Come to see your dad the mayor in action?"

"Something like that."

He nodded toward the stage. "Who's that beside Molly?"

Charity stood on tiptoe and scanned the crowd. "That's Abby Walsh. She's a good friend of Molly's and mine. Those are Jamie Gibson's parents on Molly's other side. Jamie's another good friend. I wonder why she's not here. Usually she's right there with the other two."

"How come you're not down there rounding out the fearsome foursome?"

She met his gaze. "The real question is, why aren't you down there? Sitting with Molly."

"How's that?"

"Oh, please, Mr. I-want-to-borrow-coffee. Or was it sugar?"

"That obvious, huh?" He stuck his fingertips in the pockets of his jeans.

"Yeah. You need to think of something smoother, then work real hard at keeping your story straight."

"Yes, ma'am."

"Oddly enough, it makes me like you."

"Excuse me? I win points because I can't remember my own made-up story?"

"Yeah. It means you're not so smooth."

He'd been fresh out of smooth ideas to get Molly's attention. She'd been avoiding him at the preschool and he hadn't seen her around the apartment complex—not for lack of looking. He'd found her apartment number by checking out her name on the mailbox and going to her place had been the spontaneous result of his frustration. And his timing had been excellent since she'd needed a man. He'd been happy to oblige. But he'd be happier if he could get past her wall of reserve and find the warm and nurturing Molly Preston he'd seen painting with her preschoolers. That woman was someone he wanted to get to know. Correction: know again.

But he didn't want to share his problem with Charity. So, it was time to change the subject. "How come you're not up there with your father?"

She frowned. "Baxter Wentworth doesn't need my help. He does a fine job as auctioneer. Besides, he ordered me to keep a low profile."

"Because?"

"I'm a publicity magnet, and I'm not talking the good kind." She studied the assembly, gesturing to the few empty seats available. "How come you're not sitting? Are you hanging in the back for a quick getaway?"

"No. The truth is, I've never been to the auction." When he was growing up, every cent had gone for survival. There hadn't been any left over for charity. They could have used some, but his father was either too proud or lost in the bottle. Des was curious about the philanthropic side of Charity City. "I'm here to check out how it works."

She rolled her eyes. "Like I believe that. It's all about ego. You just want to see who's going to buy you and how much they'll pay."

"Busted." He grinned. "Can't blame a guy for being curious. If someone's not willing to put up more than a dollar and a half, it could be humiliation of the public and personal kind."

"I don't think you have to worry."

"A guy always worries." Money affected everything—including love. He'd had a big lesson that opened his eyes.

"What?" he said, when he saw the gleam in her eyes.

"At the risk of feeding your ego, there are numerous women who would pay a lot for a good-looking hard-hat hunk like yourself. But I have a hunch one in particular has you on her shopping list."

His ears had been burning after his botched coffee run, and he hoped she meant Molly. "Who?"

"Just wait and see," she said mysteriously.

The microphone crackled, signaling that the short break in the action was over. The mayor reminded the audience that it was a milestone anniversary of the auction and he was counting on everyone to make it the most successful one ever.

Charity nudged him and whispered, "That's just a small taste of the rah-rah pep talk Jack and I have been getting because we were born Wentworths."

"It's a worthy cause," Des reminded her.

He remembered Molly's passionate support for the preschool expansion in order to provide more children with an early education.

The mayor announced that there were three "guys" left to auction—the first being Des O'Donnell, who was donating a home repair. Des happened to be watching Molly during the proclamation and saw her elbow the woman beside her and whisper something. Maybe Charity was right about Molly's intention to bid on him. The idea pleased him because he'd enjoy the opportunity to spend some time with her.

An opening bid was announced and the auction started. Each member of the audience had been issued a number to hold up when they wanted to push a bid higher. Des was surprised when Abby Walsh did just that. Around the room, people—mostly women—cranked up the amount.

Charity rubbed her hands together and grinned. "All right, O'Donnell."

He wasn't going to the ego place. Whoever bought him knew they were getting a home repair. It wasn't as if they were expecting money and social prominence from him and would walk away when he didn't provide them. Like his fiancée had. But darned if the price of him didn't keep going up, although not on account of Molly. She didn't raise her number once, but he noticed another round of lively whispering between Molly and her friend.

Finally the mayor banged his gavel. "Sold to the little lady in the third row."

Des frowned at Charity. "So why couldn't you tell me Abby Walsh intended to buy me?"

"Because I didn't know. That was a surprise." Charity's forehead puckered as she stared at her friends. Then she shrugged and looked at her program. "The next guy up for auction is a retired LAPD detective. Sam Brimstone."

"Not a hometown boy? How did he get talked into this?" Des asked.

"The goodness of his heart?" But Charity's grin told him there was more to the story.

When the bidding on the detective was over, Roy and Louise Gibson had purchased his services.

"I wonder what the Gibsons want with him?" Charity mused.

Before Des could comment, the mayor announced the final guy for auction: Riley Dixon of Dixon Security, who'd donated a survival weekend. There was another round of vigorous bidding and by the time the mayor banged his gavel, Abby Walsh had once again beat out her competition.

"After you get that home repair taken care of," the mayor said to her with a wink, "you can get away from it all for the weekend."

Looking surprised, Charity folded her program. "I wonder what Abby wants with two men?"

"Maybe a home repair and a survival weekend?" he suggested.

"Very funny. And very curious. She's a single mom

on a budget who just coughed up a lot of money. Even when you factor in the tax deduction…" She shook her head.

Des didn't really care. He'd do his duty and fix whatever he was told to fix. But the woman who'd bought him wasn't Molly. And he found that pretty doggone disappointing. In fact, the depth of his regret convinced him that it was a very good thing she wanted nothing to do with him.

Chapter Four

Molly took a deep breath and knocked on Des's apartment door. Heart pounding, she waited for him to respond and swore her life flashed before her eyes. As lives went, hers wasn't pretty. But she was about to do something about that.

Suddenly the door opened and Des's eyes widened in surprise when he saw her. Then he smiled. "Molly. To what do I owe the pleasure?"

He owed her plenty, she thought. But pleasure? Maybe not so much. "May I talk to you?"

"Sure," he said, stepping aside for her to enter.

She glanced around his apartment, noting its different layout from hers. Most notably, there was no dining area. The living room was furnished with a chocolate-brown leather sofa and love seat—very expensive, if she wasn't mistaken. A big-screen TV dominated the wall across from the sofa. And the beige walls were bare. Another difference between them.

"So, what did you want to talk about?"

She turned to face to him. He must have showered after work, because his thick, dark wavy hair looked slightly damp and the scent of soap mixed with a spicy cologne made her pulse jump. He smelled way too good and his worn jeans and black T-shirt did a number on hormones that hadn't had much to get excited about lately.

"Could we sit down?"

"Sure." He held out his hand, indicating the sofa. "Sounds serious. Should I be worried? Is this another time-out moment?"

"No. Nothing like that."

Her laugh sounded nervous and she hated that it did. Best get this over with. She sat on the love seat and sank into the soft, supple luxury. Fortunately, he sat on the sofa, so at no time did any parts of their bodies touch.

Molly folded her hands in her lap. "As I'm sure you're aware, last night was the Buy-a-Guy auction."

"Yeah." He leaned back and rested one ankle on the opposite knee, a purely masculine pose. "I was there."

"You were?" She hadn't seen him. But she hadn't been looking. Most of the guys didn't show up since their presence wasn't required and the buyer would contact them later.

"I was standing in the back with Charity Wentworth.

She gave me a running commentary on the proceedings. I haven't heard from Abby Walsh yet about what kind of project she has in mind for me to do."

"She doesn't have anything in mind."

"Oh?"

Molly twisted her fingers together in her lap. "That is, she probably has a great many things in mind. But none of them involve you."

"But she had the highest bid."

"Yes, I'm aware of that. But she wasn't bidding for herself."

He frowned. "Then who?"

"She was doing my bidding."

"You?" He didn't look like he was ready to make gagging noises. Mostly he just looked surprised.

"Me."

He shrugged. "I don't get it."

"What's not to get?" His services being bought and paid for should be familiar territory to him. But this time she'd been the one buying. "Abby bid. I wrote the check."

"But your father is Carter Richmond, as in Richmond Homes. He's the biggest builder in the area. Surely if you had a repair that needed doing he could get a crew here in a heartbeat and it wouldn't cost you anything."

Molly went rigid. Of course, her father was in a position to help Des professionally which explained why going out of his way to be nice to her probably had less to do with the preschool expansion than his own business expansion. Why hadn't she thought of that before?

Her oversight had to be the result of channeling all her energy into resisting her attraction to Des. And her resistance was a dismal failure.

Even now. Even realizing that his howdy-neighbor-can-I-borrow-some-coffee visit was calculated, she could easily swoon over the gleam in his eyes and fall victim to the sin in his smile.

Once a user, always a user, it seemed. Volunteering his crew for Buy-a-Guy had probably been part of his plan, she realized. History had taught her that he was all about Des. She'd learned the lesson well. She knew what he was capable of and wouldn't be so gullible this time. Forewarned was forearmed.

"So why buy a home repair when your father's in the business?" he asked again.

Molly took a deep breath. "I wouldn't ask my father for something like this."

"I see." He leaned forward. "You paid a considerable amount for my services. Apparently preschool teachers make some big bucks. Or does Daddy supplement your income?"

The implication that her father was still paying anything on her account pulled her stomach into an angry knot. She wouldn't take anything from the man who'd orchestrated her humiliation. In fact, she'd made a point of not even discussing the bribe with her father. All she wanted to do was put the manipulation behind her and make sure it didn't happen again.

"Teaching gives me some income, but it's more a

labor of love. I have a trust fund from my mother, who died before I was thirteen, which makes me completely independent from my father. He paid for college. But now I wouldn't ask him for anything."

"Hmm. I bet Carter Richmond had a few choice words to say about that."

"I doubt he noticed. At the time he was too wrapped up in wife number two—the trophy." Gorgeous Gabrielle. It was only a guess, but Molly was pretty sure her stepmother had put her father up to paying Des to date her in high school. Heaven forbid Carter Richmond's daughter embarrass his new wife. She would never forgive them—her father for interfering, Gabrielle for urging him on. Or Des for being a willing participant.

"I sense some hostility."

"No, I—"

"That wasn't a criticism, Molly. I think your independence is a good thing."

"You do?"

He ran a hand through his hair. "Look, no one knows better than me that fathers can be a pain."

"How would you know?"

"Mine was an alcoholic."

"I didn't know, Des. I never met him. That's why you never went to your house. I'm sorry," she said, sincerely meaning it.

He shrugged, but his eyes hinted at a mother lode of painful memories. "It's in the past. The point is, I think we both have issues with our fathers."

"So?"

"It gives us something to bond over."

Assuming she wanted to bond. Which she didn't. But the revelation took some of the starch out of her resentment. And wasn't that just a darn shame? There wasn't a whole lot except resentment standing between self-respect and making a fool of herself over him for the second time.

Now for the hard part. "About the reason I bought you—"

"Yes. My curiosity is at fever pitch."

His curiosity. Her hormones. Like mixing sparks and gasoline. She wished she didn't have to bare her soul, but there wasn't any other way.

"I bought you to be my escort for the Charity City High School reunion festivities," she said in a rush.

For the second time since he'd opened the door to her he looked genuinely surprised. "But why?"

So many reasons. All of them humiliating. "Do I have to explain?"

"No. Well, just one thing. Why would you pay so much for me?"

"It was for a good cause?" she answered lamely.

"But guys are probably lined up around the block to take you out."

"Not really." Damn that little glow starting in her belly. "But maybe that's because word got out that I beat guys off with a stick."

He laughed. "The truth is, Molly, I'd have taken you to your reunion even if you hadn't bought me."

"Well, I don't know what to say."

Recently, he'd told her she was a knockout. And the geeky adolescent still lurking inside her desperately wanted to believe he meant what he'd said. But Molly had believed him once and paid a high price. Not in money, but in self-esteem and trust.

"Now that's settled," he said, "can I get you something to drink? Soda? Coffee?"

She blinked at him. She'd made a deal with the devil—or rather, she'd bought and paid for devil-may-care Des. And he'd agreed to her terms. But she needed to guard her emotions carefully. To do that, she needed to go. There was no staying for social stuff.

But she didn't know how to exit gracefully. She was bad with men. Or was Des the only man she had this problem with?

"I'm not thirsty." She stood, then remembered her manners. "Thanks anyway, but I have to go. School stuff. I'll be in touch about the reunion."

And only the reunion.

She hurried to the door and let herself out.

When Molly left his apartment so abruptly the night before, Des would have sworn she'd kill a bug with her bare hands before contacting him until it was absolutely necessary. She'd shocked his socks off with her announcement that she'd purchased him to be her reunion date. The pretty lady was one big surprise package, complete with red hair and more curves than a mountain road. He thought he'd have to wait until the reunion to see her, but she'd left a message on his cell that she needed his help at her apartment. So here he was.

She answered his knock in seconds. "Des, come on in. Thanks for coming over. Trey is here. There was an emergency. His mom was in a car accident. Nothing serious, but the doctor wanted her admitted to the hospital overnight. I brought Trey home with me because she had no one to take care of him."

Des remembered Molly telling him the boy's father was out of the picture. So marshmallow-hearted Molly had stepped up. She was definitely a soft touch. For Trey. For the auction committee. For everyone, apparently, but him.

"Your message said you needed help. What can I do?"

"Is that Des?" A child's voice sounded down the hall, followed by running feet. Then Trey was there, grabbing him around the legs. "You're here. Finally."

Des ruffled the boy's curly hair, then squatted in front of him. The child's face was freckled and round, and his blue eyes were shadowed. "Hey, buddy."

"Did Miss Molly tell you? My mommy's in the hopspittle."

Des nodded solemnly. "I heard. Miss Molly said she's gonna be fine. You doing okay?"

He nodded. "But Miss Molly says visiting time is over."

"The hopspittle has rules," Molly explained, humor

shining in her green eyes. "He talked to her on the phone, though."

Trey nodded. "She said she loves me and she's gonna miss me. But she'll prob'ly be home tomorrow."

"Good." Des stood, but kept his hand on the boy's shoulder.

"And Miss Molly made me a hot dog because it's my fav'rite dinner."

"Sounds good," Des agreed.

"Oh, gosh, Des. I didn't even think. Have you had dinner?"

He shook his head. "Your message said it was important. So what's the emergency?"

"Miss Molly bought me a building set. But I can't build nothin'—"

"Anything," she corrected.

"Anything. My house keeps fallin' down."

Molly shrugged. "I stopped off at the toy store and bought him something age-appropriate, according to the packaging. But apparently they lied. Who knew it took a postgraduate degree in construction to build it?"

"And Miss Molly says she only played with dolls. She doesn't know nothin'—" he stopped and looked at her "—anything," he corrected, "about building. But I 'membered you build stuff. And she said she'd call, but you were prob'ly busy."

"I was," he said, noting the pink in Miss Molly's cheeks. "But I'm not now. Let's see if I can help."

Trey held his hand and led him to the spare room

where snap-together blocks were strewn around the floor in front of the spare twin bed. "There's nothin' to nail. Or hammer either," Trey said, rubbing a knuckle under his nose.

"Sometimes you don't need tools." Des sat on the floor and picked up the directions. "Let me look at this. Builders usually work from a blueprint."

"Builders need energy," Molly said. "Would you like a hot dog?"

"Miss Molly makes really good ones," Trey added.

"Yes," she agreed. "They're world-famous. Chefs everywhere are green with envy over my hot dogs."

Des grinned at her. "Then how can I say no?"

After he ate, the three of them spent the next hour building a castle. Des watched the way Molly lavished attention on the child to keep him from thinking too much. Des had a hard time keeping his attention on the blocks and off her mouth and how much he wanted to find out if it was as soft and sweet as it looked. Finally, Trey yawned and curled up on the floor between them.

"That's a cue if I ever saw one," Molly said, standing. "Time for a bath, big guy, and a quick bedtime story."

"Do I hafta?"

"Yes."

"Will you read me a story?" he asked Des.

"You bet."

"Okay." Trey stood and took Molly's hand. "I can take a bath all by myself. Fast. Don't go away," he said, pointing at Des.

"I wouldn't dream of it."

They left the room and Des's thoughts turned to Molly. In her classroom, he'd seen first-hand her soft spot for children. The fact that she'd consented to call him, of all people, because Trey needed help building was more proof of how much she cared. But that didn't mean her capacity for caring included him.

He wondered, and not for the first time, if her wariness of him was because she knew about the deal he'd made with her father. But surely she would have said something. It was a "time-out" offense for sure.

Carter Richmond hadn't said anything about Molly knowing when Des recently presented him with the detailed bid for the new housing project. Of course, part of the deal with Carter was that the truth remain their secret. Des had complied—except for one person. He hadn't meant to say anything, but Kelli had guessed the truth during a fight. But she and Molly had hung out in completely different crowds. It was unlikely their paths would have crossed. Besides, with a summer in between, by the time school started again it was old news.

Des had changed a lot since high school. He wasn't that immature jerk who would juggle two girlfriends and he wanted Molly to know that. He wanted an opportunity to show her the man he was today. To build a friendship with her.

"I'm ready for my story now." His hair damp and freshly combed, Trey stood in the hall wearing Bob the

Builder pajamas and holding the ragged teddy bear Molly had brought from his house, where a neighbor with a key let her in. "Miss Molly made me a bed."

The words Molly and bed in the same sentence lit a fire inside Des and visions of tasting her mouth roared through his head again. But Des pulled himself together and helped tuck the boy into the guest room bed, story and all.

After kissing the child good-night, they quietly left the room and went to the kitchen. Des leaned back against the island.

"Kids have a lot of energy. My hat's off to you."

"Your hard hat?" she asked.

He laughed. "Yeah. I guess I made a connection with him that day at school. You were right about how powerful a drop of attention is to a child starved for it."

She stood in front of him. "I'm guessing your grandfather gave you more than a drop of attention since he started teaching you to work with wood when you were about Trey's age."

"I can't believe you remembered that."

She lifted a shoulder. "Go figure."

"You're right. My grandfather took me under his wing when I was just a little guy. He knew what my father was even then, and he picked up the slack."

"You were lucky to have him."

"Tell me about it. And yet, building wasn't what I wanted to do originally. I tried a different career path. Bond trading. Made a lot of money at it, too."

"And yet now you build things."

"Yeah." He folded his arms over his chest. "There's something satisfying about working with your hands, building something from nothing that's lasting and good."

"You gave Trey a taste of that tonight," she pointed out.

"Until you made us take it apart and put it back in the box."

"Yeah. Sorry about that. But I didn't want Trey sleeping in a construction zone. A trip to the bathroom during the night could be a safety hazard."

He laughed. "No kidding. But I suppose construction is in my blood."

"Even so, why abandon a lucrative career?"

"I'd been thinking about it for a while. Missed working with my hands."

"What tipped the scales in Charity City's favor?"

"My dad died. And my mom needed help running the business."

"Is she still involved?"

He shook his head. "She stepped in out of necessity, but never really wanted the responsibility. I took over and she retired. She's visiting her sister in Florida to see if she wants to live there."

Molly's eyes went soft with approval. "You made it possible for her to have choices."

He blinked, aware that he'd spilled his guts. He didn't normally do that. He kept his personal information personal. But there was something about Molly that made him comfortable talking to her. Maybe it was the knowledge that growing up with a father like hers couldn't have been easy. If he had it to do again, he'd tell her old man to take a flying leap. But in the here and now, he was feeling a little sheepish about running off at the mouth.

He rubbed the back of his neck. "It's always a plus not to be between a rock and a hard place. Choices are good."

"You're a good son." Molly stared into his eyes and smiled with genuine warmth for the first time since he'd seen her again.

Suddenly he was no longer sorry he'd spilled his guts to her. Not when she looked at him like that, with her good opinion of him shining in her eyes. She was pretty before, but a smiling Molly was a downright stunner. Then he looked at her mouth. The lips that had been tempting him since that day in her classroom curved up and became his downfall.

He simply couldn't stop himself from sampling her sweetness.

Chapter Five

Molly knew she should put a stop to the kiss, but then she'd have to give up the mind-blowing sensation of having her body pressed to his, his heat and strength, not to mention the spicy scent of male surrounding her. And the way his mouth devoured hers. The blood surged to her head, squeezing out rational thought. And along with rational thought went her reserves of will-power. Needs, so long dormant, snapped to life and surged through her system.

Liquid heat collected in her belly, then bubbled through her, leaving a trail of fire in its wake. She linked her arms around his neck, then slid her fingers into his hair. In his throat he made deep moans of approval that turned her on even more.

His eyes were dark and fiery as he met her gaze just before he brushed his mouth across hers in a single, sexy stroke that turned her inside out. He nestled her sensitive breasts to the solid wall of his chest and her nipples tingled as she rubbed against him, aching to be touched. Yearning grew inside her, spilling into all the lonely, empty places.

He gripped her hips, then slid his hands up her sides as he kissed her—long, slow, deep. She let the taste of him slide over her tongue, a taste she remembered from years ago, then slowly absorbed him into her system. Her head spun and her body churned as the thrill of this moment hummed through her. The thrill cranked up when his wide hands barely brushed her breasts, making her breath catch.

All she could think about was the smell, touch and taste of Des. The years melted away as remembered sensations came to life again. But this time they were stronger. She was a woman now, not a girl. She had a woman's responses to a man's touch and the need was more. So much more.

No one before or since made her want the way Des did.

"Miss Molly?"

The child's voice pulled them apart in a nanosecond.

Molly refused to look at Des as she took a deep breath. "What is it, Trey?"

He stood in the hallway rubbing his eyes. "Are you kissin' Des good-night? My mommy always kisses me good-night."

"I'll tuck you back in," she said, moving toward him. "Thanks for coming by, Des."

Molly welcomed the distraction to rein in her runaway desire. What in the world was wrong with her? She'd been so close to throwing caution to the wind. And there was a child under her roof. Besides, she knew better. She'd been dumped on twice, and to give dumper number one a second shot at her was simply too stupid for words. As she settled Trey into the bed again and read him another bedtime story, her pulse calmed and her skin cooled.

"It's getting late, Trey. You need to go to sleep."

"I miss Mommy."

She brushed the hair off his forehead. "I know, sweetie. But the sooner you go to sleep, the sooner time will pass and she'll be home from the hospital."

He looked at her with large, solemn eyes, then nodded. "Miss Molly?"

"Yes?"

"How come you were kissin' Des?"

It had been too much to hope he'd forgotten. "You were right. He was just saying good-night."

"Oh." He rolled onto his side.

"Good night, sweetie," she said, bending over to brush a kiss on his forehead.

"I'm glad Des kissed you good-night," he said. "My mommy says without a kiss it's not good-night."

"Right." Her night would have been way better without Des's kiss. She was grateful to this little guy for

bringing her to her senses. If he hadn't interrupted...
"Sleep tight, sweetie."

Molly tiptoed from the room and pulled the door
almost closed behind her. After letting out a long breath,
she walked down the hall to the living room, and
stopped short.

"Why aren't you gone?" she said to Des.

He was standing in her kitchen, arms folded over his
chest as he leaned against the island. "We need to talk."

That was the last thing she wanted to do. "I don't
mean to sound ungrateful—"

"Which means you're going to say something that
will sound suspiciously like that."

"Please go," she said abruptly. She walked past him,
careful not to get too close as she moved to open the
door and see him out.

He reached to curve his fingers around her arm
before she could do that. "Why are you ticked off?"

"Who says I am?"

"You did. And I quote, 'Why aren't you gone?' And
'Please go.' On top of that, hostility is building in you
like the storm surge after a hurricane."

"You're imagining things."

And she thought she'd been so cool. Would he buy
her bluff and hit the road? She was behaving ungra-
ciously after he'd come so promptly when she'd asked
for his help. If only he hadn't kissed her. That had
opened up a Pandora's box of emotions, leaving her raw.
She didn't like the feeling. If he kissed her again, she

wasn't sure she could resist the powerful temptation his special brand of masculinity presented.

"I don't have that good an imagination." Intensity burned in his blue eyes as he looked at her. "Now quit dodging the question and tell me why you're angry."

Pulling her arm free of his fingers, she stepped back. She needed to establish a perimeter around herself, an intimacy-free safe zone. Folding her arms over her chest, she held his gaze. "I'm mad at myself."

"That's different. Usually you're mad at me. What did *you* do?"

"I'm an idiot. And I hate that I am."

He gestured toward her sofa. "Can we sit down?"

"No."

"Okay. Then let's get right to the point. How do you figure you're an idiot?" he asked.

"You dumped me when I was a chubby high-school kid who wore glasses and had braces on her teeth. And I asked you to come here tonight."

"You did that for Trey." Something flashed in his eyes, then his gaze narrowed on her. "But as far as high school—that was a long time ago. I'm not that same self-centered immature jerk. I've grown up. And so have you."

Appreciation smoldered in his eyes, but she did her best to ignore it. She wouldn't get sidetracked again. "Here's the thing, Des. It really doesn't matter to me what you're like now. Relationships are highly overrated. Intimacy isn't what it's cracked up to be.

I'm not attracted to you that way. Or anyone else, for that matter."

"That's not what your kiss said."

Her heart pounded. Again, bluffing seemed to be the response of choice. "And what exactly did my kiss say?"

"That you were experiencing a high degree of interest."

She stuck her hands into her jeans pockets, stalling for time as she chose her words. "I'm sorry if that's the message you got."

"That's the message I got because it's the vibe you were giving off."

"It wasn't intentional."

"I know."

"You surprised me."

"I surprised myself." One corner of his mouth turned up. Only Des O'Donnell could look sheepish and rakish at the same time. Go figure.

"Surprise," she said, throwing up her hands. "Anyway, I just don't want either of us having any expectations. That could get awkward."

"As opposed to what we're experiencing now," he said.

"Right. Well, I'm glad we cleared that up."

"Right."

"So there are no misunderstandings," she said as she made her way to the door and opened it. "Thanks for coming by, Des. I know it meant a lot to Trey. Good night."

He hesitated and she prayed he wouldn't drag this out. His animal magnetism was alive and well and having its way with her. If he decided to push his advantage, he'd expose her declared noninterest for the bald-faced lie it was. She needed time and distance to put her defenses firmly in place before the reunion just a few weeks away.

"I'll be in touch about the reunion activities."

"Okay." He walked out. "Good night, Molly."

She smiled and waved, then shut the door. Progress, she thought. She hadn't shut it in his face. Maybe she was getting better at dealing with men.

Tell that to her hammering heart and sweaty palms. Her SOS tonight had been about making a scared, lonely little boy feel more secure, which they had done. Only, she'd proven how *in*secure she still was with Des. What delusion had made her think she could handle being around him for a whole weekend?

But there was no turning back. To back out now would reveal her foolishness and she wouldn't be made a fool again—not this time.

Des walked the new cement-slab foundation of the preschool wing, checking for anything amiss. The construction site had been fenced off to keep anyone, especially the kids, from accidentally wandering into the hard-hat area. Because his crew wasn't scheduled to start framing for a day or two, he was surprised to hear footsteps behind him. He thought it might be Molly and eagerness rushed through him. He hadn't seen her for a week, not since he'd kissed her. He turned and frowned.

"Wrong Richmond," he muttered to himself.

Des wondered how an unfeeling, manipulative man such as Carter Richmond could have raised someone as warm and nurturing as Molly. He remembered Molly telling him that her mother had died before her thirteenth birthday, so maybe she'd had enough positive influence from her mom to make her the person she was.

"O'Donnell," the other man said in greeting.

"Richmond."

Des remembered being intimidated by Richmond as a teenager, but those days were behind him. They were nearly the same height, but Des had the older man by an inch or two. Richmond won in the dapper department, Des's jeans and work shirt no match for Richmond's expensive navy pin-striped suit and silk tie. Richmond also had a lot more silver in his hair now.

"Nice work so far," he said.

"Thanks." Glancing at the cement slab, Des felt a rush of pride. He'd supervised everything himself and made certain all materials were up to code and the workmanship as perfect as possible. The foundation was reinforced with rebar, but there was no way Richmond could know that.

"I had you checked out."

"Is that right?"

"Your bids are fair. Good quality workmanship. No corners cut. Punctual, particular and tidy. Your reputation is stellar."

"Good to know."

"No thanks to your father."

The jab hit home, just as the bastard intended. But Des wouldn't let him see. "From the time my grandfather founded the company until the day he died, O'Donnell has been a strong name in construction."

"If that's true, why did the Wall Street whiz kid come home?"

He wouldn't have asked if he didn't already know, telling Des that Richmond had dug really deep when he'd checked him out. Know your opponent's weakness. "I accomplished everything I wanted and got bored."

"So you came home to rescue the family business? To undo the damage your father did and restore the company's good name?"

Anger grew inside Des, bright and hot. This man had once used his family's misfortune against him. While working summers at O'Donnell Construction, Des had taken a second job with Richmond Homes. The company had a scholarship program for Charity City High School seniors and Des had applied. During his interview with Carter Richmond, the older man had offered to increase the scholarship award—*if* Des would date his daughter and ensure her acceptance by the high school in-crowd.

Des had been between a rock and a hard place. He hated being poor and knew education was his only way out. But college cost money his family didn't have. And student loans wouldn't necessarily cover the bill.

So Des had made a pact with the devil. And lived to regret it.

"Why did I come home?" he repeated, weighing his answer. "It had a lot to do with challenge. I had all these business skills I'd acquired. And I had a love of the construction business that my grandfather instilled in me."

"Ah."

The response was noncommittal and the expression in the older man's eyes was guarded, making Des wonder. Did Richmond know how much of his own money Des had pumped into the family business to rescue it?

"What are you really doing here?" Des asked.

"My daughter works here."

Carter Richmond didn't give a damn about Molly. If he had, he wouldn't have interfered in her life the way he had all those years ago.

"Yeah. But you're not here to see Molly, are you?"

"No." He laughed. "You're sharp. Always were. The money I spent on your college education wasn't wasted."

Des winced. "I work hard. At anything I do," he added.

"I like you, Des. Always have." His eyes narrowed and he stuck his hands in the pockets of his suit slacks. "But you don't like me."

"Can't say I do."

Richmond nodded thoughtfully. "You're honest. I like that, too."

"Okay." If the man was waiting for him to suck up,

Des figured he could stand there until Texas got snow in July.

"The fact is, I'm here to check out your work for myself. I've narrowed the slate of candidates for the building contract to two—and O'Donnell Construction is one of them."

Des didn't react one way or the other, not wanting the other man to know how relieved he was at the news. Again, he decided there would be no sucking up to tip the scales in his favor. Either he'd get the contract because he was the best man for the job, or he wouldn't get it at all. But he wondered if the old man knew how much O'Donnell Construction needed the contract to build the new housing development. The company was limping along, but a juicy project like Richmond Homes would give it a much-needed infusion of capital.

It was déjà vu all over again. The man had bought him once; but it wouldn't happen a second time.

"So, I guess you've seen my daughter since starting this job."

Not only had he seen her, Des had kissed the living daylights out of her. His body stirred at the memory

"Yeah, I've seen Molly," he answered evasively. And she'd shut him down, for which he should be grateful.

"She's grown into a lovely young woman."

No thanks to this guy. It was all Molly. "She always was a sweetheart."

Now she was a hot sweetheart. But Des didn't want

to go there. After that amazing kiss, she'd claimed re-
lationship-shyness, but it was her way of letting him
know that he wasn't good enough for her. Or more spe-
cifically, guys like him who dump girls in such a
careless way don't get second chances.

Somehow Des had expected Molly to be different
from his fiancée. When he'd agreed to her father's bribe,
he'd told himself it was okay because she was a rich girl
and all about money. She wouldn't get her feelings hurt.
Then he'd gotten to know her and found the sweet,
funny girl who'd been down to earth and not into
money. Since Molly, he'd only once trusted a woman,
but he'd trusted her enough to propose marriage. That
had lasted until he'd shared his dream of returning to
his roots in construction, then Judy had run far and fast.
Her message came through loud and clear: she hadn't
loved him. She'd only cared about his success and his
money. Without either he wasn't good enough for her.

"Look, Mr. Richmond, it's been fun, but I've got
work to do. Punctuality comes with a price."

"Meaning you can't stand around and socialize with
a son of a bitch like me."

"Your words, not mine."

He nodded his approval. "Very well. I'll be in touch."

Des watched him walk away and realized those were
the last words he'd heard from Molly. Like father, like
daughter? They'd both bought him. Carter Richmond
was a scheming manipulator and seemed to take pride
in the fact that he was. Des had trouble believing the

same about Molly, but he couldn't afford to take the chance.

She hadn't followed her father into the family business, but Carter had raised her. How much of him had rubbed off on the impressionable girl she'd been? Molly had said it best. *Fool me once, shame on you. Fool me twice, shame on me.*

He would meet his obligation. He would accompany Molly to the reunion. But he didn't plan to let her get close. No matter how much he wanted Molly, he wouldn't be taken in by a woman ever again.

Chapter Six

Football in Texas was practically a religion, which made the Charity City High School homecoming game the perfect kickoff for the reunion activities. As Molly followed Des into the bleachers, spectators were bobbing and weaving to see the field as they searched for the perfect vantage point. Of course, Molly wasn't concerned about the view of the game. It was all about being seen.

Des stopped at a row three-quarters of the way to the top, picking a spot with barely enough room for two in the center of the bench. Way to draw more attention to us, she thought, disturbing half the row as they took their seats. No one in that section, possibly the entire stadium, could miss the fact that she was with Des O'Donnell.

Her last time in these bleachers, Molly had been a sophomore with a crush bordering on worship for the captain of the football team. After learning he'd been paid to date her, she hadn't attended another game. Until now. Ironically with Des as her date.

A few weeks had passed since that night in her apartment when he kissed her, and she hadn't been able to think about much besides the way Des's mouth felt pressed to hers. How good it felt to be snuggled in his arms.

Then she'd seen Des talking to her father at the preschool, bumping his kiss to number two on the Top Ten list of things she couldn't get off her mind.

When Carter Richmond was involved, she had to wonder about Des's game. He wasn't calling the football plays now, but she had to wonder if he was playing her—again. This time things were different. She was no longer a young girl with a thing for the bad boy on campus. Now she was all grown up and that leveled the playing field.

As they settled on the cold metal bench, she tried to keep any part of her body from touching any part of his. But every time Des moved, his muscular thigh brushed hers, threatening to send her up in flames. Her heart pounded as if she were the player who'd just run the football in for a touchdown.

"Well," she said brightly, "here we are."

"So, what am I supposed to do?" Des had the twinkle in his eyes that signaled trouble.

"Excuse me?"

"As your escort… What do you expect? You bought and paid for my services, so—"

"Shh." Finger to her lips, she glanced around to see if anyone had heard.

He followed her gaze, then looked at her, one eyebrow arched. "The plot thickens. Obviously, the fact that you purchased me at the auction isn't for general publication."

She glared at him. "Say it a little louder. There's probably someone in Oklahoma who didn't hear that."

He grinned. "Discretion is my middle name."

"Really? I thought it was Sean." Darn. Would he read anything into her remembering his middle name?

"You know what I meant."

"Yes." She sighed and hoped it sounded long-suffering instead of relieved. "But I'm a little nervous."

"No," he said, exaggerating surprise. "I'd never have guessed."

"Look, Des—"

A cheer went up and from the hometown crowd, and Molly figured the Charity City Cheetahs had done something good.

"What?" Des asked, leaning close.

Good for the team, bad for her, she thought as his closeness made her stomach jump. Her heart, just settling down, started hammering when his warm breath stirred strands of hair around her face. A cold front had moved in, sending the night-time temperature into the fifties, but suddenly she wasn't cold.

She swallowed. "I'd prefer no one knew the particulars of our association."

"Why is it so important to you to have a date this weekend?"

Not just any date, she thought. The guy every girl had lusted after in high school. The bad boy who made school worth getting out of bed every morning and sitting through boring classes on the off chance of seeing him—even from afar. Once upon a time, he'd made her life exciting. But she was prepared to tell him none of that. Still, he deserved an answer.

Unfortunately, she had to enlighten him in public. Keeping her voice down meant getting chummier than she'd anticipated.

"In high school…" she began.

"Yes?"

She moved closer and he bent his head to hear, cranking up her heart rate even more. "When I walked the halls of Charity City High, there were some girls who weren't very nice."

"It happens."

"Not to you," she pointed out. Especially with girls. "I'm pretty sure you were never voted the face most likely to stop a clock."

The sympathy shimmering in his blue eyes said he knew she meant herself. Then his expression turned dark and brooding. "I wonder if anyone gets through high school without regrets."

"Probably not," she agreed. "But the thing is, I have

to go to the reunion. The teacher who mentored me is retiring and it's important to me to honor her. I've been dreading going back, and Charity Wentworth suggested that having a date might make the experience more palatable."

"So you got Abby Walsh to do your bidding for a date so the mean girls wouldn't know why you bought my services."

"Exactly."

"Okay." He nodded. "Now that I've got my motivation, I'm going to need a little direction."

"How's that?"

"This is your how-do-you-like-me-now moment. Do you just want me to be arm candy?"

She blinked at him. Arm candy? For her? "I don't know—"

"Or do you want hands-on displays of affection?"

The very idea of his hands on her started a shiver inside that had nothing to do with the cold. "I guess I hadn't thought about th-that."

"The thing is, Molly, there are different ways to play this to make it work. But I need to know what your expectations are." He looked terribly sincere, until the gleam in his eyes gave away the fact that he was toying with her and enjoying it immensely.

But she could see his point and replied, "I'm not really sure how to behave. Isn't it enough that I'm here with you?"

"If I were you, I'd want jaws to drop."

She smiled. "That works for me."

"Okay. But if we're going to make that happen, we need to look like a couple. We need to act like we're sincerely and intimately involved."

"Oh." Oh boy! She was beginning to see what he meant.

"If we're going to make this look real, it's going to mean touching. A lot of it."

"Right." Wrong. This was everything she'd been trying to avoid since he came back to town.

"And probably kissing, too."

"Uh-huh."

No. No. No! She had to think this through. She was getting in way over her head, with no life vest in sight.

"So, you understand that it makes a difference what sort of point you're trying to make?"

"Yeah. But I don't want to make you uncomfortable."

His grin was wicked as he put his arm around her and snuggled her to his side. "I just want you to get the most bang for your buck."

"You're doing a fine job," she said, holding herself rigid.

"Relax. This will be more convincing if you don't look like one of your preschoolers just painted the walls of your classroom black."

He rubbed his hand up and down her arm. Fortunately she wore a coat with several layers of clothing underneath to ward off the cold. Surely all of that would protect her from his make-believe assault on her senses. She had to remember that this was only pretend. But as his big, callused hand slid up and down her arm, she could swear the heat of him went clear through to her flesh.

As if stroking her wasn't enough, he lifted a finger and tucked her hair behind her ear, then touched his mouth to her neck, making her draw in a quick breath against the tingles dancing over her skin. Lord help her, he knew he had her, but she liked being had.

If only she could go back to thinking of him as the heartless jerk who'd used her. But learning his father was an alcoholic made her look differently at the young man he'd been. She realized that beneath his veneer as football hero and big man on campus, he was a boy with flaws, frailties and feelings. He was human, although it was dangerous for her to think of him that way. Because he'd hurt her once, and if she didn't toughen up, he would again. It wasn't a hardship to relax against him and smile—for the benefit of anyone who could be watching, she told herself. She was glad Des had thought to put on this front. But then she'd bought herself the guy who'd once totally pulled the wool over her eyes then broke her heart. A sad sigh slipped out and she hoped it looked appropriately adoring.

Another sigh escaped because this was going to be the longest weekend of her life.

* * *

As they rode the escalator to the second floor of the Adams Mark Hotel, Des kept his hand at the small of Molly's back. Her skin was like silk just above the plunging back of her black dress.

After crossing the enclosed pedestrian bridge that spanned the street below, they entered the huge reception area adjacent to the ballroom where the reunion was being held. A registration table was staffed by women decked out in their finest. When they reached the front of the line, a blonde smiled at him. "Des O'Donnell. You haven't changed a bit."

He had, but it was all on the inside. He looked at her name tag. Nicole Burns. He hadn't a clue who she was, so he couldn't say whether or not she'd changed. "You remember Molly Richmond—now Preston," he said. "I'm with her."

Blue eyes widened in surprise as she studied his companion. "Molly Richmond? Wow. You *have* changed."

"I'm going to take that as a compliment," Molly said, smiling graciously, although he felt her stiffen under his hand.

Des studied Molly's face and admired her poise. No one would guess that she'd been dreading this.

Nicole hunted through the card file in front of her and produced their name tags. "You're all set," she said, smiling brightly.

"Thanks." Molly turned to look up at him. "I'm just going to the ladies' room to freshen up."

"I'll wait for you."

As Molly began to walk away, behind him he heard Nicole say to the woman beside her, "I had no idea mega-Molly would show up. Did you see who she came with?"

"Des O'Donnell," someone answered in a loud whisper. "She's way more forgiving than I'd be."

"No kidding." Another loud whisper. "Everyone knows her father bought Des for her in high school. She knows it, too. Why would she come with Des O'Donnell, of all people?"

Des watched as Molly stopped, then turned, her jaw clenched in that determined way of hers as she walked back to the front of the line. "I came with Des because he's my date."

"Did your father arrange it?" Nicole asked.

"Actually, no. He no longer interferes in my life. However, I'm grateful to him for bringing Des and me together in high school." She smiled brightly at him. "We've developed a terrific relationship over the years."

"That was obvious." Nicole sniffed. "Judging by the two of you necking at the homecoming game last night, may I say, get a room."

"We did actually. I'm sure there's a good reason the reunion committee picked a place an hour away from Charity City. But for those of us going to Mrs. Tobin's retirement tribute tomorrow, it was inconvenient to drive back and forth." A look of satisfaction blazed in Molly's eyes. "So I made a reservation here at the hotel.

And I'd like to say to you what I should have said to everyone in high school."

Nicole's chin lifted in a stuck-up and self-important way. "What's that?"

"Bite me."

"Miss Molly, you are really something." Des put all the respect and admiration he felt for her into the grin he beamed her way.

Her own smile widened. "As are you." Then she met Nicole's gaze again before shooting a defiant look at the woman beside her. "I've never been happier."

Des nodded. "I couldn't have said it better myself."

It wasn't easy taking his cues from her because he was still reeling from the fact that she'd known all this time what he'd done. But his hat was off to her. She'd stood up to the mean girls, and she'd done it with intelligence, class and dignity.

He nestled her to his side and smiled down at her. "Have I mentioned how stunning you look tonight?"

"Yes," she lied. "But a girl never gets tired of hearing it."

"You take my breath away." And he was telling the honest-to-God truth.

"Thank you," she said, a becoming blush stealing over her cheeks.

"Now, I believe you mentioned freshening up. Not that you need it," he added.

"Right." She nodded to the women behind the table who looked shell-shocked. "Nice to see you all."

With his hand still on her back, Des felt Molly shudder. Immediately, he propelled her away from the registration table and toward the restrooms.

When they stopped, she stepped away from him. Only then did he see the shadows in her eyes and the strain in her expression. She'd pulled it together brilliantly, but that ugly scene and her show of bravado had cost her big-time. And it was all his fault.

"Molly, why?"

"Why, what?"

"If you knew what happened, why did you want me to be your escort? You had to know that was coming."

"It would have happened whether you were with me or not." With a trembling hand she tucked a strand of red hair behind her ear. "It was easier with you as my date. I don't think there was a girl at Charity City High who didn't have a crush on you. Every one of them wishes they were in my shoes. And you're with me tonight."

"But why—"

"I don't want to talk about it. Let's just let the past die. I want it buried and that's what tonight was all about for me."

"I respect that. But I still think we need to talk about it—"

The squealing of the public address system cut him off. He glanced over his shoulder and spotted Mike Weber, an old football buddy, with the microphone. Mike announced that he'd been designated master of ceremonies and had a list of messages—deletions in the program, activity time changes and general announcements.

When Des turned back to Molly, she was disappearing into the ladies' room, but not before he saw the pain in her eyes, a hurt that went clear to her soul. What had she gone through after he'd left town? Based on what he'd just witnessed, he could only guess at the humiliation Molly had suffered.

Des was furious. Molly had said some girls in high school were mean to her. Now he knew that explanation was extremely charitable. The girls had been bitches and hadn't changed a bit. If Nicole Burns were a man, he'd pop her one.

But most of his rage was reserved for his part in this. He hated what he'd done and would give anything to take back the pain he'd caused Molly. No wonder she had been so hostile that first day at the preschool. She'd tried to pass it off as annoyance for getting her name wrong. For not remembering her. And the truth was, he hadn't recognized her because she'd broken out of her cocoon and turned into a breathtakingly beautiful butterfly. But now he knew there had been more. She'd been face-to-face with the guy who'd caused her misery and humiliation.

Now he understood why it was so important for her to have an escort to this circus, but he couldn't help thinking she'd bought the wrong guy. She'd said it helped having him by her side, but it seemed to him he'd only added fuel to the second coming of her humiliation.

There must be some way he could make it up to her. Some way to really give Molly her how-do-you-like-me-now moment. She'd said all of the women wanted to be in her shoes, the one on his arm.

She'd announced that she and Des had developed a terrific relationship over the years. Almost the truth, he thought. Recently they were good together. What if he took it up a notch? Right here in front of everyone who'd taken cheap shots at her through the years.

He crossed to the other side of the room. "Mike?" The big, dark-haired former linebacker grinned at him. "Des. Good to see you. How the heck have you been? I heard you came back to Charity City."

"Yeah. I'm running the family business." He stuck his hands into his pockets as an idea formed. "Look, since you're making announcements—"

"What?" Mike asked, looking wary.

"I was wondering if you could do me a favor."

"Maybe."

"I have a very important announcement." Des glanced around and motioned for his friend to come closer so he could discreetly whisper something in his ear.

Wariness disappeared as Mike grinned approvingly. "That's great. You got it, buddy."

Des returned to the spot where he'd been standing, waiting for Molly to come out of the ladies' room. When she did, he gave Mike the sign and his friend nodded.

The microphone crackled again as Mike put it in front of his mouth. "And last but definitely not least, I have breaking news to report. Desmond O'Donnell and Molly Richmond Preston are engaged to be married. Join me in congratulating the happy couple."

Molly's eyes grew wide with surprise as she stared at him. "What in the world have you done?"

Chapter Seven

Shock didn't begin to describe what Molly was feeling. Was someone making fun of her? Was their charade working too well? Or did she need to hunt down the rumor monger and stomp the living daylights out of their gossip network?

Suddenly there was a crowd around them and Des was shaking hands in response to the congratulations being bandied about.

Nicole Burns approached her. "Why didn't you say something about your engagement?"

"I didn't know we were making it public yet." Way to land on your feet, Molly congratulated herself. Go with the flow and all that.

"Des must be excited. He couldn't have picked a

more public place to make the announcement. Let me see the ring." Nicole grabbed her hand, the left ring finger conspicuously naked.

Oh, great. If she blew this, Des was going to rue the day he thought up this stupid plan. "I don't have one yet. It's all been pretty sudden."

Nicole shook her head, disbelief lurking behind her smile. "Nice going, Molly. Landing Des O'Donnell is the stuff of legend."

"That's me. Legend girl." She nodded in his direction. "Excuse me. I have to go see my fiancé now."

Why should everyone be so astonished that she could land the legend? Then again, no one could be more astonished than she. Molly felt as if she'd awakened in a cockeyed version of Rip Van Winkle, except she hadn't gone to sleep and she'd only been absent ten minutes.

Finally she worked her way through the throng surrounding Des to his side. "Miss me, darling?"

"I missed you something awful. But I always do when we're apart." His grin, full of the devil on charm pills, was mocking her.

"Funny you should mention that. I can't leave you alone for a minute."

"I'm lost without you, Molly." He knew she knew what he'd done and was really laying it on thick.

And then he gathered her into his arms, no doubt getting into his part. But darned if her body didn't have a mind of its own as the blood pounded in her head and her breath caught. He nuzzled his lips close to her ear and when the resulting tingles subsided enough for her to think straight, she heard him whisper only for her to hear, "Just play along."

Then he bent her back, supporting her with his strong arms as he kissed her thoroughly. Cheers, whistles and applause erupted from the crowd surrounding them, but her hammering heart nearly drowned out the noise. Her senses were still spinning when he straightened her and settled his arm around her waist, keeping her possessively against his side. That was a good thing, because without his support, she'd have melted at his feet like chocolate in a fondue.

Whatever game he was playing now, God help her, she liked it. She felt like Cinderella at the ball doing her thing in the glass slippers. And what was the harm? This time she was in on the gag; they both knew it was pretend. So she'd play along and when it was over, she'd move on with her heart intact.

Des offered her his arm. "Shall we go in to dinner?"

"I'd follow you anywhere," she said, settling her hand in the bend of his elbow. Then her words sank in and she realized how desperately close to the truth they'd been even though she knew this was make-believe.

His trademark grin faltered for a second, then returned as brilliant as ever. "I'm a lucky man."

Near the center of the large ballroom they found their table. The centerpiece—greens interspersed with yellow mums and carnations—reflected the school colors and rested on a white linen cloth, laden with silverware enough for eight people.

Des held her out chair, then took his seat beside her. The rest of the spots were taken by people she didn't recognize. Then servers started delivering bread, salads and beverages and the resulting noise level made introductions impossible—even with the people on either side of them. All they could do was smile politely at one another. Molly wasn't prepared to answer questions about her and Des and was grateful that meaningful conversation was out of the question.

The din rose even more when the lights dimmed and a slide show began on two enormous screens bracketing the stage. It was a montage of high-school moments and more than one slide featured Molly wearing glasses, smiling for all the world to see her ugly braces and the short haircut she'd thought would make her pixie-like, but instead gave her an elf-look. And not the cute Christmas kind.

She leaned over and whispered to Des, "Whoever is responsible for that slide show, I want you to beat them up."

"Okay," he said seriously. "But I have to go on record that I think you were cute."

"Oh, please. You're so lying."

He put his palm over his heart. "As God is my witness. But the fact is, back then, everyone was like an awkward puppy growing into their feet."

"Not everyone. You were always smooth, together, and all parts of your body in the proper proportions."

"All parts?" he asked, one eyebrow arching.

Her face grew hot. "I couldn't say."

He leaned close and whispered. "I wasn't so together, Molly. If anyone knows that, it's you."

She met his gaze. "Des, I—"

"No matter what you think, high school wasn't easy for me." An intensely serious expression darkened his face.

She knew he was talking about his deal with her father, but this wasn't the time or place to discuss it. Fortunately she was spared the need to respond as Mike Weber took the microphone and started his opening remarks with some joke about Mike with the mike. Then he introduced various former class officers who related anecdotes about popular classmates.

Molly hadn't been one of them—except for the time Des had paid attention to her. It had been nice while it lasted, before she learned the truth. Before she'd become fodder for jokes.

But she was with Des tonight. And his announcement of their "engagement" felt like a protective bubble that would deflect insults, barbs and jabs. She felt safe with Des.

Even so, when the music started, signaling the dance portion of the evening, she hesitated when he stood and held out his hand.

"Shall we?"

Ooh, he was good at this, she thought. Looking into his blue eyes with their bad-boy gleam and feeling her insides quiver at the charming grin directed at her, she could almost believe that this was real. If she took his hand, he would guide her to the floor where a slow dance was in progress. A waltz required her to be in his arms, with her body pressed to his from chest to thigh and at the mercy of her hormones. If she refused, their charade could be exposed, leaving her wide open for humiliation all over again. The whole point of buying his time had been to avoid embarrassment.

She couldn't dance with him and she couldn't refuse—the definition of messed up. It was a no-brainer. Come on, Molly, she thought. Grow a spine.

She put her hand in his and smiled so everyone could see what an outstanding orthodontist she'd had. "I'd love to dance."

Well done, Molly, she thought—until he put his arms around her and drew her close to his hard body. Then he settled his warm palm on her bare back. Only then did she realize the folly of this little black dress that revealed as much as it concealed. She'd hoped to make his jaw drop, along with everyone else's. Something dropped, all right. Her heart, hitting bottom at the brush of his fingers over her exposed flesh. Her breath caught and she stepped on his shoes.

"Sorry," she mumbled.

"Don't be nervous," he said. "I've got your back."

That was the problem—his warm fingers stroking the exposed skin up and down her spine. "I can't help it."

"Just try to relax."

Easier said than done, she thought, as he wrapped her fingers in his hand and pressed her closer. He smoothly circled them around the crowded floor while familiar faces from her past whirled by. The mean girls smiled and told her she looked fabulous. Time had been good to her. She looked beautiful. Her first thought was always that they were lying and she wondered why the bad stuff was so much easier to believe.

As Des whirled her past the stage, Mike Weber tapped him on the back. Des stopped, his arm automatically encircling her waist.

"Hey, buddy. Leave it to you to be with the prettiest girl in the room."

Des glanced down at her. "I got lucky."

"Isn't he a charmer?" Molly said.

Mike nodded. "I hardly recognized you."

"Is that good?" she asked, trying not to go to the bad place.

"Definitely. Who knew the freckle-faced carrot-top with the bad haircut in those pictures would grow up hot enough to melt in your mouth."

"In case you didn't hear the announcement," Des said sarcastically, "she's engaged, Mike."

"You had to remind me," he said regretfully. Then a gleam stole into his eyes. "I just remembered something. Isn't your father the president of Richmond Homes, Molly?"

"He is," she said, feeling Des's arm tighten momentarily.

"And Des is running his family's construction business." Mike nodded as he looked at them. "Convenient. A match made in heaven."

"She's an angel, all right," Des said.

"No kidding. If I'd known you'd turn out this good, I'd have paid more attention to you in high school." He slid her an admiring look. "Mind if I cut in?" he asked Des.

"Yeah. I do. I'm the jealous type." The words were light, but his tone wasn't.

Tension emanated from him as he whisked her into his arms and danced away. A glow grew inside Molly. Was he really and truly jealous? Then the glow sputtered and fizzled out as she realized he had no reason to be. Mike held no appeal for her. No one could hold a candle to Des. He was the only one she wanted. And how stupid was that?

He'd proven he could put on an award-winning performance. If she forgot it was an act, he could break her heart again, and she had no one to blame but herself.

Recognizing the problem was half the battle. Now she had to figure out a way to win the war.

Des waltzed Molly toward the French doors that led onto an outdoor balcony, the soft romantic lights surrounding the outside enclosure pulling him like a magnet. He had an intense desire to have her all to himself, and the dance floor had become way too public. Even though she was sweet torture in his arms, seeing her in *another* man's arms would be torture of the not-so-sweet kind. He'd felt white-hot rage when his old buddy had come on to her—an engaged woman. Or so everyone believed. Des hadn't been prepared for the jealousy that roared through him…or the insinuation that he'd asked Molly to marry him because of the business her father could send to O'Donnell Construction. Mike had been way off base. In fact, the only thing Des had agreed with was that Molly was the prettiest girl in the room.

The prettiest girl who probably thought he'd concocted the phony engagement to suck up for business reasons.

Once they were outside, she yanked her hand from his and pushed against his chest to free herself. "You've got some explaining to do. I leave you alone for five minutes and we're engaged? All I wanted was a date to this reunion and I wind up with a fiancé. What's up with that?"

"It's called redemption."

"I need a couple more details," she said, folding her arms beneath her breasts.

He forced himself to ignore the interesting things the pose did to the plunging neckline of her dress. "I could use a few of those myself. Like how long you've known about my deal with your father."

She released a long breath that ended with a sigh. "After you'd graduated…when school started again…

your girlfriend told me—and the rest of the school. Generous of you to share the gag with her."

"It wasn't like that, Molly."

"Oh? What was it like?"

"She was jealous of you."

"Oh, please." She shook her head. "I didn't just fall off the turnip truck. Jealous of *me?* You can do better than that."

He'd have been skeptical, too, until a few minutes ago when the green-eyed monster tweaked him. "I can't do better than the truth. I was spending a lot of time with you"

"For which you were well compensated," she said, her chin lifting proudly.

"Okay. The thing is, Kelli didn't share well and we had a fight about you. Things were said. She guessed—"

Molly held up a hand. "Don't tell me. She said something like you wouldn't go out with mega-Molly unless someone paid you."

That was pretty close, he thought, but the last thing he wanted was to throw salt in her wounds. "Like I said, things were said. Then I broke it off. I might not be the sharpest tool in the shed, but I knew I didn't want any part of someone so shallow and possessive."

"You forgot cruel and vindictive."

"That, too." He ran his fingers through his hair. "Look, Molly, you have no reason to believe this, but when I got to know you, I genuinely liked you. If I had a do-over, no way would I have hurt you like that."

"My father made it all possible."

"I won't argue with you about that. But it doesn't excuse what I did." Des stuck his hands in his pockets because he so badly wanted to pull her into his arms and erase the shadows in her eyes. "It's important to me that you know why."

"Okay." She folded her arms beneath her breasts again.

He swallowed as he held her gaze. "I told you my father was an alcoholic. But the problem spilled over into every part of his life, personal and professional. Because he was unreliable, business began to fall off. His reputation went to hell. There wasn't enough money to pay the bills, let alone pay for college. And that was my ticket out." He took a breath. "And I wanted out, Molly. I wanted it bad—any way I could get it."

"So education was your Achilles' heel."

He nodded. "I worked part-time for Richmond Homes and applied for the company scholarship. As you know, one of the decisive factors in awarding it is an interview with the president of the company."

"Which was when my father found out your weakness."

"Right again. When he offered to increase the scholarship in exchange for making sure you were friends with all the 'right' people, I didn't think twice. I grabbed it."

"There was no other way?" she asked in a sad little voice.

"Not that I could see."

"What about football? Or an academic scholarship?"

"I was a good player, but not great. My grades were decent, but not outstanding. I was one of those students in danger of falling through the cracks. And I'll admit state school or junior college were less-expensive options, but I wanted to get away from *him*. The only thing I had going for me was my determination *not* to be like my father."

"Oh, Des—"

The hand she put on his arm mocked as much as it comforted. He pulled away. "I don't want your pity. It's just a fact of life. My dad was a failure on every level. So I hated when he said like father, like son. He never missed a chance to remind me that I wouldn't amount to anything. Just like him."

"And you did what you had to to keep that from happening."

"I don't expect you to understand, Molly. But that's what happened."

"You certainly proved him wrong." She caught her top lip between her teeth. "Did it ever occur to you that he provoked you to make sure you took a different path from him?"

He shook his head. "Interesting theory. And if you're right, it's a hell of a bad parenting technique."

"It worked."

"I suppose. But I didn't care who I had to step on to get away from him. All I knew was that education was my ticket out of his life."

Molly sighed. "I had no idea what you were going through. You told me recently he had a drinking problem, but didn't let on how abusive he was."

"It's over. He's gone. I only told you so you'd understand and maybe forgive me someday." He was surprised how important it was to him that she did.

"I forgive you right now."

The sweetness in the smile she gave him warmed him clear through. "Even though I was the reason girls were mean to you? Then I wasn't there to run interference?"

"The teasing and taunting weren't the worst."

Hard to believe. Tonight, he'd seen a glimpse of what she suffered as a vulnerable, sensitive girl. "What was worse?"

"Finding out my father thought I was such a loser that he resorted to buying me a social life."

"Did he say it like that?"

"I wouldn't know. We never discussed it."

"You didn't tell him he could take the social life and shove it?" He wished she had. Even though it would have meant losing his college fund. He hadn't breached the secrecy portion of his agreement with Carter Richmond but the bastard wouldn't have cared. Des still would've lost out.

Molly shook her head. "It was too humiliating to talk about. Hurt too much to know he didn't think I was okay just the way I was. Aren't fathers supposed to love their children just like they are?"

"You're asking the wrong guy." He laughed, but it was a bitter sound. "My father was nothing but a cautionary tale."

"For what it's worth, I think my stepmother had something to do with it. Gorgeous Gabrielle was always after me about my hair and clothes. 'Appearance is everything,' she always said. And she told me the Richmond name carried responsibility. I always felt I was a blight on the name we shared. What hurt was that I was a Richmond by birth. She married into the family, and that carried more weight."

"There was nothing wrong with you, Molly." Funny. Now he was the one doing the comforting.

"I got through adolescence," she said. "But college took me out of the frying pan into the fire."

"What happened?"

"I fell for a computer geek. Unfortunately, I missed the warning, 'The guy behind the glasses is more shallow than he appears.'"

He laughed, marveling at the way she could make light of her past. She was really something. Plucky as well as pretty. "You married him?"

"How'd you guess?"

"Your last name changed."

"Oh. Right. After I married Bruce—" she shuddered "—I found out he didn't think I was thin enough, because with every second helping came a judgmental look along with a reminder about my waistline. And then there were the comments that with all my money I could afford LASIK surgery to get rid of my glasses."

"And?"

"How did you know there's an 'and'?"

"Bad things always seem to come in threes."

She nodded. "It's the last bad thing because it was the last straw. He suggested breast augmentation."

It was as if someone warned him not to look at the accident on the side of the road. To save his life, Des couldn't have resisted looking at the barest curve of her breasts revealed by the low-cut neckline of her dress. The fleeting glance was enough to make him wish they were somewhere private so he could separate her from her sexy dress and get a good look at the sexier body he knew was inside it.

"You do know Bruce was an idiot. Probably still is."

"Even if you're lying, I appreciate the sentiment." Molly met his gaze and shivered.

He shrugged out of his jacket and draped it around her shoulders. As hard as it was to cover something so beautiful, he didn't want her to be cold. He left his hands on her arms and looked into her eyes. "I'm not lying."

It would have been easier if he were. He'd liked her years ago, but now there was even more to like. If he could let himself chance it. She'd said earlier that she'd follow him anywhere. But he'd been burned by someone who wouldn't follow him because she considered the construction business beneath her.

An address, profession or clothes didn't make the man. And Des wanted to be loved for the man he was. The problem was, Molly knew the man he'd been and likely wouldn't give him another chance. That should make him think twice about starting anything with her. But he was standing in the moonlight with a beautiful woman and thinking was the last thing he wanted to do.

"It's probably time we checked into the hotel." Her voice held a hint of breathlessness. "I—I mean our rooms. Separate rooms. Which is what I made the reservation for."

She was right. They'd put in another appearance, very publicly acting like a couple. Just one night alone in his room and one more day and his escort services would no longer be needed. The thought didn't bring him as much comfort as it should have.

"Okay," he said. "Let's call it a night."

Chapter Eight

They'd called it a night, but the hotel wasn't letting Des follow through on his good intentions. As yet, he didn't have a room—some reservation mix-up. So, while he waited, he carried Molly's overnight bag to her suite.

"Sweet," he said, glancing around. The sofas and chairs were elegant. The wood of the tables, desk and dining-room table and chairs was a dark, rich cherry. Brass lamps were everywhere and a crystal chandelier in the foyer dripped sparkling light on the marble floor. "Is my room like this?"

Molly sat on the brocade sofa and slipped off her high-heeled pumps. The activity didn't quite cover the fact that she wouldn't look at him. "First of all, with the reservation messed up, you might not have a room. Second, if it hadn't been messed up, I wouldn't have—"

"The best room in the place," he finished for her. "And I don't."

"Well… Yes," she admitted.

He leaned his forearms on the high back of the wing chair as he studied her. Take the woman out of the moonlight and a man started thinking with his head again. It was good to get a reminder that Molly was her father's daughter and accustomed to the finer things in life—no matter what she said about working for a living and supplementing that income with a trust fund. That didn't change the fact that Molly had been raised in affluence and probably wouldn't adapt well to a lesser lifestyle. Because if his business tanked, he'd lose everything.

He recognized the expression on her face as guilt. "Forget it, Molly. You bought my time. Staying over in the hotel is a convenience. I don't need much."

The expression on her face changed and he recognized it. It was concern. She'd looked at Trey that way when she'd been taking care of him. That was Molly. She nurtured, and seemed to enjoy doing it.

What would *she* have done if he'd told her he was turning his back on a high-powered career to work with his hands? Would she have sucked it up and walked away from the New York nightlife so that he could find the satisfaction he craved in resurrecting the business his grandfather had started? Would she have loved him for himself if he hadn't done her wrong all those years ago?

What did it matter? He wasn't likely to take a chance with her again. And she wasn't likely to give him one.

The clock on the desk chimed midnight and Molly glanced at it. "I wonder how long it will take registration to find a room?"

If he didn't know better, he'd think she was nervous. But he knew for a fact that women weren't always what they seemed. Although she looked sweet and innocent, she was undeniably sexy. That dress. Her curves in that dress. Her red curls tumbling around her face. It was the perfect storm of sexiness.

Molly was hot, all right, and Des knew that in spite of his hard lesson from a high-maintenance woman, he wanted Molly in his arms and in his bed. Which technically he didn't have yet.

"At least we have somewhere besides the lobby to wait while they check on it. Are you sure you don't want to go home and come back tomorrow for the tribute?" he asked.

When she shook her head, her red curls seemed to catch fire in the light from the lamp beside her. "It's late. Charity City is over an hour away. That's a lot of driving. I'm sure they'll find something. It's just a matter of time."

She ran her tongue over her lips and he nearly groaned. Apparently moonlight wasn't required for a

man to start thinking with other parts of his body. And
he wasn't the only one thinking that way. Molly was
talking too much, a sure sign of nerves. And he couldn't
say he was sorry that the feeling was mutual.

Molly saw the way Des's face grew tense and his
eyes dark. He took off his suit coat and dropped it care-
lessly in the chair, then loosened his tie and rolled the
sleeves of his white dress shirt up to just below his
elbows. She didn't think it was possible for him to look
sexier, more masculine. Unless he was in jeans, boots
and a tool belt.

She'd thought when they retired to separate rooms,
she'd get a break from working so hard to resist him.
But that hadn't happened yet. And when he looked at
her like that…

"So tell me," she said.

"What?"

"About yourself."

He slid his hands into his pockets. "You already
know about me. I didn't spill my guts enough tonight?"

She'd seen traces of the desperate young man he'd
been, and wished she hadn't. Sympathy wasn't her
friend. It would only lull her into letting down her
guard, which would be a disaster. She glanced at the
phone and prayed he would have his own room soon.

She pulled herself together. "I don't mean that part."

"I'd rather hear about you."

"Speaking of spilling one's guts—you know all

about me and Bruce the Bottom-feeder. Tell me what happened after you left Charity City. I know you went to college."

"Yes, and after, I worked in New York as a bond trader."

"Sounds exciting. Bright lights, big city. And I remember you saying you were good at it."

He grinned. "Oh, yeah."

"So small-town boy makes good. Proves father wrong." She tapped her lip. "Boy comes back to Charity City, leaving the excitement of the big city."

He looked as if someone had just hosed down his day planner. "It wasn't all exciting."

"New York?"

"Go figure," he said, shrugging. "Anyway, it got old and I needed a challenge. I always liked working with my hands."

"Good grandfather memories?"

"Yeah." The dark look lifted and a soft smile curved his mouth. "That and Charity City is growing fast. It seemed like a good place to find the challenge I was looking for and set new goals. Along with using the skills my grandfather taught me."

"What about personal?" She couldn't believe those words came out of her mouth. But now that they had, it was clear that she desperately wanted to know.

But his frown was back and it seemed as if he wasn't going to answer. Finally he said, "There's not much to tell."

"*Not much* means there's something to talk about."

"Are you going to drop this?" His deep voice had an edge.

"I might have, except your reaction tells me I shouldn't drop this on a bet because there's something interesting."

"Not to me. But if you must know, I was engaged."

"To be married?" she blurted out. The announcement hit her squarely in the midsection and she barely held in a gasp of surprise. Which was dumb because she shouldn't be surprised. Women would be all over Des O'Donnell like nerds on the latest computer.

"Is there any other kind?" he answered, one corner of his mouth curving up.

"Wow. Marriage… That's a little more than not much to tell. And I'd be happy to read between the lines, except you're not giving me any lines to work with. What happened?"

"I didn't get married."

Molly wanted to shake him until his teeth rattled but she noted the wide chest and broad arms and figured he was too big. She wanted his personal life to not matter to her, but obviously it did. So again a question she couldn't suppress popped out.

"Why didn't you marry her?"

His mouth pulled into a straight line—a dead giveaway that his stubborn streak was kicking up. But before she could decide how to pry the information out of him, the phone rang. Molly answered and unfortunately the news wasn't good.

She hung up and looked at Des. "That was hotel registration and the inn is completely full. Apparently a lot of the reunion people are staying over."

"Okay." He started pacing. "I could find Mike Weber and bunk with him."

"That's a good idea," she said.

He thought it over for several moments. "No, it's not."

"How come?"

"We're supposed to be engaged. How would it look if I left you and bunked with a guy?"

"Like you're gay." She started to giggle.

"Very funny." His mouth curved up in a half smile. "Our engagement would look like a hoax."

"It is," she pointed out reasonably.

"No one else is supposed to know that." He stopped pacing and stared down at her. "For better or worse, we have to look like we're engaged. Now that I think about it, this is probably for the best."

She caught her bottom lip between her teeth. "You think?"

"Yeah. The odds are slim, but what if someone found out we had separate rooms?"

"I see your point."

"Look, Molly, they're not going to get another shot at you. Not on my watch. And I wouldn't do anything to hurt you. Not again." He paused. "But this is your call."

She didn't have much choice. He was right. And she didn't want to give anyone another shot at her either.

"This is a big room. I think you should sleep here."

Except with all the hormones humming between them, sleep would be nothing more than a pipe dream.

Des opened his eyes and couldn't figure out where he was. Light was coming through a small separation in the curtains. Then he moved and his back punished him for sleeping on the sofa in Molly's suite.

"Not so sweet," he muttered, rolling onto his side.

Just then, the door to the bedroom inched open and Molly tiptoed through the living area, obviously trying not to disturb him.

"I'm not asleep," he croaked.

"Oh," she gasped, pressing a hand to her chest. "Good Lord, you startled me. I'm sorry I woke you."

Me, too, he thought, unable to take the high road and ignore the almost transparent peach satin nightgown she was wearing that molded to every peachy little curve on her body. What was a man to do when she was backlit in the doorway? Her red hair was tousled from sleep and surrounded her face like a fiery haze. God help him, she looked two parts purity and one part sin.

A man could only take so much and he couldn't suppress a groan. Bad move, he thought. She was kneeling by his side in a heartbeat.

"Des, are you all right?"

"No." Unless wanting her so much he hurt made him all right.

She touched her small, cool hand to his forehead and

he wanted to imprison her wrist and press his lips to her palm. "Are you sick?" she asked. "Do you need a doctor?"

He removed her hand and, for a moment, held her small, delicate fingers in his own. "I'm not sick."

"Then what's wrong?"

"I'm having a hard time keeping my hands off you."

Stunned, she sat back on her heels. "You are?"

"I am, yes." He released her and sat up, sliding his feet to the floor before folding his arms over his chest. His boxers wouldn't go a long way toward disguising his reaction to her. "In fact, keeping my hands to myself with you kneeling there, looking like that, is probably just about the hardest thing I've ever done in my life."

"It is?"

She sounded pleased and that didn't improve his mood.

"Yeah. I should get a Boy Scout badge of honor."

"I'll see if I can find one," she said, a breathless note in her voice.

"Don't bother. I'm no Boy Scout and what I'm thinking is anything but honorable. You better go in your room right now and shut the door. And lock it."

Molly stared at him for several moments and the pulse in her neck fluttered wildly. Then she smiled as if she'd just realized something. "Oh, I get it. This is part of the pretend engagement and you're getting back into character."

"Okay. Sure. If you say so."

But his body wasn't pretending anything. His nerves were strung so tightly, he was about to snap and tug her into his arms. "You better get moving. Don't we need to get ready for the tribute?"

"I'll be quick," she said, standing.

She moved away, taking her warmth and sweet scent. He missed her already.

Through the closed bedroom door he heard the shower and got an instant visual of a naked Molly, red hair slicked off her forehead and fanned over her bare shoulders, white satiny skin sleek with water. The image of her with her head wantonly thrown back, small, firm breasts thrust forward, made his palms ache to touch her.

Des groaned again, but this time only he heard. Then he buried his face in the pillow and tried to sleep. Although why he should be successful now when he'd tossed and turned most of the night, he couldn't say.

What seemed like a lifetime later, Molly opened the door. Her hair was pulled away from her face and twisted into a sleek knot at her nape. She was wearing a long-sleeve, high-neck knit dress that covered a lot more skin than her nightgown, and he was more grateful than he could say.

Until she walked over and turned around. "Can you get this zipper for me? It's stuck."

Des stood. In front of him was all that creamy fair skin he'd imagined—not wet, but disturbed only by the thin line of her virginal white bra. One flick of his wrist and he could see everything he'd just imagined. But they were only pretending.

Des was glad she couldn't see his hands shaking when he reached out, careful only to touch her zipper and not the tempting flesh just millimeters away. It wasn't easy, but he managed not to graze her. That should count for something.

She turned and smiled up at him. "Thanks. Do I look okay?"

If *okay* meant that every luscious inch of her was highlighted to perfection, then yeah, she looked okay. He let his gaze roam from the top of her coppery hair, over her tempting breasts and slender waist, down her shapely legs to trim ankles and slim high heels. "You look amazing."

She released a breath. "Thanks."

"You're welcome."

And thank you for turning me into roadkill, he thought. A sleepless night on a hotel sofa just a few steps away from Molly and paradise did not make for a restful night. Or day either. It's almost over, he reminded himself. In a few hours the torture of Molly, so near, yet so far, looking at her and not being able to touch, would be over. All he needed to get through it was a quick, miserably cold shower.

Molly felt tingles dance through her when Des took her hand to escort her into the room where the tribute for Mrs. Tobin was being held. It was already crowded with a smaller and less shallow, but still curious group of former Charity City High School students. Like the previous night, many of them did double takes to see her with Des O'Donnell. But today, she held her head high and fortified herself with the memory of the way he'd looked at her in her nightgown, and the thread of hoarseness in his voice when he'd said he was having trouble keeping his hands off her.

But what really got her inner femininity revved up and rarin' to go was that he'd been thinking dishonorable things about her. Did that mean he wanted to ravish her? Oh, she hoped so.

But that chink in her self-control was for later. Right now she wanted to honor her favorite teacher who was retiring. "I see Mrs. Tobin over there," she said before glancing up at Des, so handsome in a charcoal suit, black dress shirt, silver-and-garnet patterned tie.

"Okay. Let's do this," he said.

They wove their way through a sea of bodies to where Rosemary Tobin sat, alone for the moment, on the dais. She was a small, good-natured brunette with remarkably few wrinkles lining her face. Dressed in navy slacks with a coordinating sweater set, she looked just like she had the last time Molly had seen her just before high school graduation.

"Mrs. Tobin," she said, leaning over to give the woman a hug.

"Molly, dear, you look wonderful."

"So do you. How are you?"

"Happy. I'm looking forward to pursuing my interests outside the classroom. And I'm pleased to see you so happy." She eyed Des doubtfully. "Des O'Donnell. I heard you two are engaged?"

"Yes, ma'am." He put his arm around Molly.

"How did that happen?"

Molly had poured her heart out to this woman when the gossip was all over school. She should have realized an explanation would be required. It was one thing to fool the mean people, but quite another to deceive this teacher who meant so much to her and knew her so well. Molly's brain seized up when she glanced at Des.

Des gave her the I'll-take-this-one look. "I'm doing the expansion project where Molly works. We got reacquainted."

"So her father didn't buy you this time?" Mrs. Tobin pushed her glasses up more firmly on her nose as she waited for an answer to her direct question.

"You have no idea how much I regret that." Des's arm tightened reassuringly when Molly flinched. "I always liked Molly in high school. We're grown-ups now, and affection and respect turned into more because *she* bought me with her beauty, her brains and the sweetest little booty in the Lone Star state. If you'll pardon me for saying so."

Relief poured through Molly as she smiled up at him. Even she believed him, and she knew he was lying. "That," she said, "is why I find him irresistible."

Mrs. Tobin nodded approvingly. "You two look very happy. I'm pleased for you, Molly. I always worried about you. Now you've got the knight in shining armor that you always wanted."

"Yes," she said, smiling up at Des. "I'm fine now."

Or she would be when they could stop pretending they were in love. If it went on too much longer, it might not be pretend. For her.

Des was surprised how easy it was to act as if he were in love with Molly. He *had* liked her all those years ago. But this time it was different, and not just because her father wasn't involved. This time he wasn't leaving and without too much trouble he could really have a thing for Miss Molly. Which wouldn't be very bright because he'd destroyed any chance with her a long time ago.

It was a relief when they were all asked to take their seats and brunch was served—the typical rubber chicken, rice the consistency of gravel, and cheesecake that sat like lead in the stomach. Then the moderator called up Molly to introduce the retiring teacher.

Des was surprised. "You're making a speech?"

"It was something I really wanted to do. And why I couldn't just blow off the reunion."

"Break a leg," he said, grinning.

"Thanks."

Molly took five-by-seven cards from her purse, then walked to the dais to stand in front of the lectern. "We're here today to honor Rosemary Tobin who's retiring from teaching, a huge loss to secondary education. She was more than a teacher to me: she was mentor and mother. If not for her, I'd never have known that a career choice isn't always about a salary. It's about working in a field you love."

Des wished he'd learned that lesson in high school. Things might have been very different for him.

"I followed her example and became a teacher," Molly continued. "But for me it's about planting seeds in the minds and hearts of preschoolers. It was Mrs. Tobin who encouraged me to ignore family pressure and find a profession that would give me satisfaction. I love what I do. And I love Mrs. Tobin. Charity City High School students are going to feel your loss." Her voice cracked as she smiled at the older woman. "I give you Rosemary Tobin."

They hugged at the lectern, then Molly stepped down from the dais and took her place beside Des. He reached out and linked his fingers with hers. When she met his gaze, there were tears in her eyes and he took her napkin to brush them away.

"I'd like to thank everyone for coming," the older woman began. "And Molly for her lovely tribute. I'll make this brief. It doesn't take a lot of words to make a point, just the right ones. Most of you were in my classes and should remember the two things I hammered into you. Every human being has dignity and matters. And all of us have a responsibility to follow our dream, wherever it takes us."

The words struck a chord in Des and he agreed with her. The only problem was finding the dream. He'd thought his involved making a lot of money. He'd done that, but hadn't found satisfaction, let alone happiness. Glancing at Molly, he noticed her discreetly wipe a tear from the corner of her eye. He felt a lurch in his chest followed by an oh-no moment. Was she part of his dream? He hoped not.

Because of their past, following her wouldn't be a good idea. Everyone remembered what he'd done to her, including her teacher. Life wasn't like a computer where you could undo something stupid with a key-stroke command. Nothing could ever delete the hurt he'd caused Molly. It was highly unlikely she would ever forgive him for his reprehensible behavior and give him a second chance.

Besides, if he ever let himself care, it would be for someone who would love him for himself, care about the things he cared about. Enough that if following his dream meant giving up one kind of life for another, she would do it because she loved him and wanted him to be happy. And it worked both ways, he realized. He had to love someone enough to give up everything.

Had he really been in love if he could so easily turn his back on his fiancée and his old life? He wasn't so sure. In fact, he wasn't sure about much. Including his belief that Molly required a privileged lifestyle. Because he was pretty sure she was the real deal.

It was a darn good thing his debt to her was done. Spending any more confined time with Miss Molly could be hazardous to his heart.

Chapter Nine

It was late afternoon when Des drove into their complex. Although Molly was tired and happy to be home, relief and regret drifted through her in equal parts. The reunion had been successful beyond her wildest expectations, but now it was over and Des was no longer obliged to spend time with her. She'd see him from a distance while he finished the preschool expansion, but their intimate time together was over.

She glanced at him as he parked the car, then stretched his shoulders. "I got through it," she said.

He met her gaze and nodded. "And without losing any fingers or toes."

"Without losing face, either, thanks to you."

"Aw shucks. Wasn't nothin', ma'am."

"Oh, please. No false modesty. Not from you. It's okay to take a bow. You were awesome. You went above and beyond the call of duty with the engagement story."

"More important, it worked. No one gave you a hard time after that."

"Nope. Took the wind right out of their sails. Mine, too," she admitted.

The steering wheel prevented him from turning completely toward her. "How so?"

"I just didn't expect it from you."

"Because of what I did in high school." It wasn't a question.

"Yes. And it was a lesson to me. Although, of all people, I should have realized."

"What's that?"

"I've certainly changed since high school. Probably everyone has and I need to be less judgmental. Cut people some slack." She shrugged. "You did something nice for me, something that wasn't part of your deal. It's a side of you I didn't know existed."

His smile was one part charm and three parts warmth. "Men don't talk about it, but we like to be mysterious. Women aren't the only ones who can play that card."

"Speaking of women…"

"Uh-oh."

"Don't get defensive. I just want to know more about the woman you were engaged to before me."

He laughed. "I'm not engaged to you."

"And pretty soon we need to leak to the Charity City rumor mill that we've broken up. Speaking of broken up—why didn't you marry her?"

"We've been through this."

She shook her head. "Not all the way through. We were interrupted by the news that you didn't have a room and had to share mine."

That news had pushed everything out of her head. It also made for a sleepless night. Like a sensual twist on the princess-and-the-pea story, she could *feel* him in the other room, breathing the same air, sharing the same space. Another experience she'd never expected to have with Des.

She stared at him, but he didn't spill his guts. "So what's the scoop? Why didn't you get married?"

"I'm not sure."

"Don't give me that."

"It was a lot of things."

"Such as?" she prompted.

"You know."

"I don't, or I wouldn't be asking. But if it would make things easier for you, I could make a list and you could check the appropriate box."

"And this list would include…what?"

"She cheated on you. She's a slob who can't cook." Molly tapped her lip thoughtfully. "She has halitosis."

"None of the above," he said, laughing. "And before you ask, I didn't cheat on her either."

"Honestly, that never crossed my mind." And it

hadn't, which told her she'd put the past away. A fact that bothered her more than a little. "So what was it?"

"You're not going to let this drop, are you?"

"It's not my current plan, no."

"Why is it so important to you?"

She realized that in their old relationship, she wouldn't have pushed because she was so pathetically grateful for his attention. The new-and-improved Molly wanted to know and had the self-confidence to ask. "I guess it's important because you don't want to tell me."

He rested his forearm on the steering wheel. "I could muscle you out of my car."

"Yeah. You could. But you won't."

"You've got my number," he said with a sigh. "Okay. Here's the breaking news. She—Judy Abbott, my fiancée—she ended it, not me."

"Oh."

Why had she assumed he'd done the breaking up? That meant he'd had his heart broken. A whole lot of breaking going on. And it was possible he wasn't over the twit—another thought that bothered Molly. More than a little.

"I'm sorry," she said. "But I feel compelled to point out that she's obviously an idiot."

"Thank you. But she's an idiot who had a good reason."

"Which was?"

"I told her I wanted to move back to Charity City. She said that was changing the rules because she'd accepted the proposal of the guy in the three-piece suit who had a high-profile job and made big bucks in the big city. Her dream had come true. She had a point."

"But?"

"My dream had changed."

"But you're still the same person she fell in love with," Molly protested.

"So?"

"I'm surprised she didn't follow you to the ends of the earth." Molly knew she would have. Once upon a time. "It seems to me that when you love someone, it's not about clothes or money or jobs or geography. It's about being with that person because it hurts too much not to be with them."

She knew because when he abandoned her, the hurt had been so great, it had taken her breath away. Wherever he'd gone, she'd have gone, too, because her happiness had been tied to being with him.

"The fact is she didn't follow me. As I remember, her exact words were that I should run, not walk, to the nearest mental-health-care professional."

"Oh, Des. I'm sorry."

"Don't be. It's over. Into every life a little rain… and all that."

Molly studied his face, looking for traces of pain from the rejection. She didn't see any, but that simply could be dusk setting in.

"I guess it's just another lesson for me. I thought your life was perfect. You're the golden boy."

"Not so much," he said. "I'm just a regular guy who puts one foot in front of the other every day and does an honest day's work—that he loves, by the way—just trying to be happy."

"Imagine that."

Just like her, Molly thought. Maybe they weren't so different. Maybe he'd changed and she could believe him. Maybe she could believe the heat in his eyes and the intensity in his kiss wasn't pretend. Maybe it was really about her and him and chemistry.

That thought brought a surge of joy so powerful, she realized she had a long way to go to get over Des. Still, she wasn't at the point of no return yet. It was a good thing he'd paid his auction debt and she didn't have to see him up close and personal.

"So, you've had experience in broken engagements," she said. "How do we get the word out that ours is kaput?"

"I'm not—"

"Because, the thing is, people will expect to see us together. As a couple. So we need to nip it in the bud and—"

"And I've been thinking," he said.

"I thought so. The lights flickered and I figured there was a power drain somewhere."

"Very funny." He grinned. "We need to let a decent amount of time pass before we leak the news that we're no longer together."

"Meaning?"

"We need to be a couple for a little while. Then we'll get the word out about our broken engagement."

"I see." How she wished she could fault his logic. But he was right. If it got out too soon, the whole town would smell a rat. "So did you have something in mind?"

"I did. What do you say to a pizza and a movie at my place tonight?"

She thought it was a really bad idea. She thought their continued pretense was too close to what she wanted as far as she was concerned. She thought she was perilously close to that place where his inevitable absence from her life would cause an emotional pain that bordered on the physical. She knew she needed distance to get back her perspective. But none of that came out of her mouth.

"I say that sounds good. I'll bring the wine."

After carrying Molly's bag into her apartment, Des was actually whistling. He wasn't sure what had put the idea in his head to invite her over, but the anticipation humming through him proved it was a good one. Even though he'd just spent over twenty-four hours with her, was it possible he'd been dreading the prospect of an evening without her?

Maybe it wasn't about hours put in. From the moment their paths crossed again, he'd realized hanging with Molly was pleasant. Bad word *pleasant*. Hanging out with Molly was so much more. It made him happy.

He couldn't remember the last time his spirits had been so high. He liked her and always had. But now he knew she didn't want relationship complications any more than he did. Which made the two of them hanging out together an even more enjoyable prospect. Just like they'd done in high school. That made her just about the perfect pizza partner.

As he drove across the complex to his place, Des whistled some more. He hadn't whistled this much since... Probably since he'd spent time with his grandfather. He'd once told Des that when a man was so full of good feelings and couldn't hold them in, whistling was the way they spilled over. Des recalled the two of them whistling a lot. His grandfather would have liked Molly, he thought, wondering where that idea had come from and why it mattered so much.

He parked, pulled his suitcase from his trunk, then took the stairs to his place two at a time. When he put his key in the lock, he found the door already open. Uneasy, he walked inside and smelled cooked food. There were dishes in the sink. "Someone's been cooking in my kitchen," he mumbled.

Had someone been sleeping in his bed?

A woman appeared in the hallway that led to his bedroom. "Hi, Des."

"Judy. How did you get in here?"

"Your apartment manager let me in." As she studied his expression, her smile dimmed. "You don't look happy to see me."

"I guess I shouldn't try bluffing in a poker game." He set his suitcase by the front door.

"A weekend trip. Anyone I know?" One dark eyebrow arched.

"A high-school reunion." He didn't owe her more than that.

She moved close and linked her arms around his neck. "Reunions are fun. I've missed you."

The feeling wasn't mutual.

Des pulled her hands away, took a step back and met her gaze. Judy Abbott was a beautiful woman—tall, trim, confident. Not even her casual jeans and white cotton shirt could soften the look. Her black hair was a little longer than he remembered; otherwise everything about her was the same—including her pale blue eyes and the slash of red lipstick on her mouth. Why hadn't he ever realized how cold she looked?

Because her eyes weren't the meadow-green of Molly's. Because Molly's red hair was as warm as the woman. Because Molly's smile welcomed and said happy-to-see-you. There was nothing especially inviting about Judy and he wasn't happy to see her.

"What are you doing here?" he asked, folding his arms over his chest.

"You're still angry."

Nope, that wasn't it. He realized he didn't care about her enough to be mad. In fact, until he'd talked to Molly about his broken engagement, he hadn't thought about Judy. Except in terms of not being so stupid again.

"I'm not angry."

"Well, I am. At myself. And I wouldn't blame you if you were upset with me, too."

"Oh?"

"I made a mistake, Des." She sighed. "Can we sit down and discuss this?"

"No."

He almost smiled when he remembered Molly telling him that in her apartment. Fortunately, they were past that. She'd told him she hadn't expected "nice" from him, and he was surprised how much a compliment from her pleased him.

Judy nodded. "Okay. We'll stand."

"It's not like you'll get tired. What can there be to say?"

Red lips pursed in a pout. "I'm trying to apologize. Letting you go was a mistake. But you need to take some responsibility, too."

"How do you figure?"

"You'd obviously been thinking about changing professions and didn't see fit to discuss it. When you sprang the news on me, I had a knee-jerk reaction that came out an automatic no."

"Okay."

She folded her arms over her chest and leaned a bony hip against the leather sofa. "But you've been gone six months. I've had a chance to think—to miss you. Maybe it was even good for us to have a separation to see how we really feel."

That was the first thing she'd said that he could agree

with. He was glad they were kaput—Molly's word. "And how do you feel?"

"I'm here, aren't I? Doesn't that say something? I followed you to see if we could find a way to work things out. Some kind of compromise."

Compromise, bargain, arrangement, negotiation, concession. Molly had said when you love someone, a job, clothes, money, geography didn't matter. It was about wanting to be with someone because it hurt too much not to be. And Judy had taken six months to decide she wanted a *compromise?* There was a time when this announcement would have been good news. But not now. Not since…

Molly.

There was a knock on the door and he jumped. That had to be Miss Molly now, here for pizza. And coming to his rescue.

He opened the door, so glad to see her he just might wrap his arms around her and never let go. "Hi."

She stepped inside. "Am I too early?"

"No. I—"

"Who's this, Des?" Judy was right behind him.

Even if he hadn't felt Molly tense, he'd have known by the startled expression on her pale face that she was upset. "Oh. I'm sorry. You've got company."

"Company? Hardly. Aren't you going to introduce me, Des, darling?"

Damn. He figured introductions were the polite thing to do even though these two had no reason on

God's green earth to interact ever again. "Molly, this is Judy Abbott."

Big green eyes grew bigger and he knew Molly remembered. They'd just talked about Judy, so he knew it was pointless to hope she hadn't remembered. But he could explain. Judy called everyone darling.

"Des and I are engaged," she said, giving Molly a cool once-over.

"Really?" Molly lifted her chin just a fraction. "Wait till word spreads that Des O'Donnell has two fiancées. It's not quite the same as bigamy, but around here news like that gets folks' attention."

Her tone was tough and together, but her beautiful, expressive face said he'd done it to her again. He'd hurt, humiliated and betrayed her.

She backed out the door, holding the bottle of wine at her side. "Excuse the interruption. You two must have a lot to catch up on. Just go back to whatever it was you were doing."

"Molly, wait—"

Without another word, she turned and walked away. Des watched her retreating figure and kicked himself for hurting her again. The fact that it wasn't his fault this time didn't make him feel any better.

"Who's your little friend? And what did she mean about two fiancées?" There was an edge to Judy's voice.

He closed the door and faced her. "I'm not going to discuss her with you. All you need to know is that you and I are over."

"You don't mean that."

"I've never meant anything more. So you can go back to New York on the next flight out."

She shook her head. "You don't mean that. You're still angry. And you're punishing me."

"You're so wrong."

"I don't think so. You and I belong together, Des."

Once maybe, but not now. He'd seen himself through someone else's eyes and he knew he was a better man than the one who'd left New York.

He ran his fingers through his hair. "It won't work with us, Judy."

"I won't believe there's not still a chance. And I'm going to stick around Charity City until you cool off and come to your senses."

"It's a free country. And I'm sure you can find a room somewhere." She sure as hell wasn't staying here.

Because when he made Molly understand what was going on, he didn't want any doubt in her mind. Nothing was going to mess things up between them. Not that he was sure what "things" between them were. But suddenly it mattered very much that he and Molly were okay again.

Chapter Ten

After her Saturday-morning exercise class, Molly grabbed her purse from her locker and left the gym. It had been a week since she'd danced with Des at the reunion—one very long, raw, and humbling week. The pressure pain in her chest proved she wasn't likely to snap out of her funk anytime soon. She couldn't believe that just minutes after telling him his kindness was un-expected and feeling that he'd turned over a new leaf, she'd come face-to-face with the woman he planned to marry. Molly had spent the last seven days telling her-self she was a fool for believing he was no longer a game-player.

Outside the double glass doors, she breathed in the fresh, North Texas air. It was a beautiful fall day and she was determined to enjoy it if it killed her. She rounded the building and stepped into the parking lot. When she stopped beside her car, she noticed a man getting out of the truck parked next to her. Only then did she notice the big O'Donnell Construction sign on the side. How could she not have noticed that sooner? And what would she have done? Jogged home to avoid him?

Maybe she could still make her getaway. After the chirp that signaled her car was unlocked, she opened the door, but before she could scramble inside, Des pushed it closed. Even as the thought made her shiver, Molly decided there should be a law against fast hands like his.

Turning, she realized they were almost chest to chest and stepped back quickly only to be rear-ended by the side of her car. Trapped by a rat.

Folding her arms over her chest, she said, "What are you doing here?"

"I need to talk to you."

"And I need to *not* talk to you."

"Sorry," he said, not looking in the least remorseful.

"Are you following me?"

He shrugged. "You brush me off at school. You don't answer your phone or your door. I didn't have any choice but to follow you."

"There's always a choice. Try taking the hint. You got it, right?"

"That you don't want to talk to me? Yeah. I got it."

He folded his arms over his broad chest and leaned his fine, jeans-clad fanny against his work truck.

"Why have you been dodging me?"

She laughed and the sound was brittle with bitterness. "Let's ignore the obvious for a second and just say that I've been waiting to deal with you until I can behave in a calm, rational and unemotional manner. In other words—like a man."

"Let's not make this a gender war."

"Oh, please. You started it with little Miss I'm-His-Fiancée."

"For starters, that's a lie."

"And based on your impeccable track record with honesty, I should believe that...why?" The sarcasm popped out, but she wasn't sorry. For some reason it made her feel in control of a situation where once she would have felt in over her head. Unlike in high school, this time she wasn't so naive, pathetic or needy.

"Second," he said, ignoring her empowerment moment, "I didn't know Judy was coming or that she'd ambush me in my apartment."

"Oh. Right. The *Fatal Attraction* defense. She's simply a nut."

"Not as far as I know. The manager let her in."

"Ah." Molly nodded but her tone said she was unconvinced.

"It's not what you're thinking."

"I'm thinking she's here. It's a no-brainer."

"She wants to get back together," he admitted.

It was surprising how deep that declaration cut. Apparently a week wasn't long enough for her heart to get the message that Des hadn't changed after all.

"Then I don't know what you're doing here talking to me."

"I'm here because you believed Judy about us being engaged."

"Why wouldn't I believe her?"

"Because she's lying. Like I told you, *she* broke off the engagement and gave the ring back. I'll admit I was ticked off at first"

"Ah, yes. Anger. The easiest emotion for a man to get in touch with. Don't you mean you were hurt? Devastated that the woman you loved turned her back?"

"That's just it," he said, running his fingers through his hair. "I should have been hurt, devastated, but I wasn't. In a very short time I knew that I'd dodged a very large bullet. She did me a favor."

"Does she know that?" Molly asked, skeptical.

"Not exactly. She says she's planning to stay in town because she thinks I'll change my mind."

"Ah."

"Define *ah*."

"It simply means that you're spinning the truth."

He had his hands on her before she could process what was happening. Lord, the man could move fast, she thought, as he pulled her closer.

"I'm not spinning anything. Here's the deal—there's something going on between you and me."

"What have you been smoking?"

"Only the fumes of what's been sizzling between us."

"Really, Des—"

He lowered his head and tenderly touched his lips to hers. Her heart hammered in her chest and the blood pounded in her ears. Her breathing went from normal to off-the-chart in zero-point-three seconds. When he broke off the kiss, they were both gulping for air.

"Tell me you didn't feel that," he rasped. "Be honest, Molly. With yourself. With me. You've been punishing me for not telling the truth. The least you can do is live up to the expectations you project on everyone else."

"I always do. And you, of all people, have a heck of a nerve throwing honesty in my face."

He dropped his hands and nodded. "You're right. Like I said, I wasn't completely honest in my past dealings with you. But it's time to write a new chapter in our history."

"And what would that be?"

"We need to honestly admit that there's something— chemistry, electricity, a connection—going on between us."

She'd felt it. But she'd thought she was the only one. She studied his face, the straight nose, square jaw, blue eyes that made a girl weak in the knees, that wonderful mouth. He looked completely sincere. But he'd looked like that when he duped the dope she'd been in high school. And at the reunion she'd begun to believe he was genuine, only to find a fiancée still in his life. Molly was afraid to believe him again.

"Why, Des?" she asked. "Why won't you let it go? Why are you pushing?"

"Because I want to see where this thing with you and me is going. And I think you do, too."

"So I'm a glorified science experiment? Electricity? Chemistry?"

"Hardly." He laughed, a deep rumbling chuckle that made her want to smile. "But I promise you this. Charity City is my home—always was, always will be. No matter what happens between you and me, I'm here to stay. And you're going to have to deal with me whether you like it or not."

He nodded, then walked away, climbing into his truck before her thought processes unscrambled enough to respond to that astounding, unsettling declaration.

Her thoughts might unscramble, but she had serious doubts about her emotions. And she wasn't sure she wanted to sort them out, because something that felt a lot like hope was bubbling inside her. Not only that, the funny little lurch in her chest signaled another four letter word beginning with L that was far more dangerous.

As soon as Trey's mom picked him up, Molly would be student-free and able to go home where there was a good possibility she'd see Des. At the thought, a ball of heat formed in her stomach and rolled through her.

Two days ago he'd kissed her. Since then, hope seemed to have a mind of its own, because no matter how hard she tried to squash it with practicality, it sprang to life inside her.

She glanced over at the little boy, content playing with cars in the toy area of the classroom. His mom was a little late and, based on past history, he might start to worry. She glanced out the window again and did a double take. She'd know that tall, silver-haired man anywhere. He seemed to be assessing the ongoing construction of what would be the new wing of classrooms.

What the heck was he doing here? He never visited her at work. When he saw her watching, he waved and headed for her door.

She remained where she stood when he entered. "Hi, Dad."

"Molly." He looked around her classroom, clearly underwhelmed. "So, this is where you work."

"Yes."

He shook his head and sighed. "You could be so much more."

Wasn't it nice to know some things never changed? Molly wasn't so sure. She was still a disappointment to him. That knowledge always stung, although she didn't dwell on it as much anymore. Bracing herself for the stab of pain, she realized it hadn't come and wondered why.

Des.

She and Des had confronted their past and put it to rest. His presence at the reunion had given her support and confidence to face her high-school tormentors. And her own father had given them the ammunition to use. She'd never confronted him because it was too painful and humiliating. Seeing her classmates again hadn't killed her, but it had made her stronger. Thanks to Des. Maybe it was past time to put what her dad did to rest, too.

"I love my job, Dad."

"Anyone could do this."

"You couldn't," she pointed out.

He looked surprised at her retort, then frowned as he glanced into the corner where Trey was putting away toys. "I have no desire to spend my time wiping snotty noses and chasing after someone else's children."

"I do. And that's the critical difference. I touch the world. I teach. I mold young minds and plant the seeds that help them grow into productive individuals. Studies have proven that children with a strong preschool background learn and progress faster in elementary and secondary education. I don't build houses, I build individuals and that's a career worthy of respect."

"I had no idea you were so passionate about your profession."

"Not surprising since you've never been very involved in my life. Except once."

His silver eyebrows arched. "What are you talking about?"

"High school. Me. Des…"

Trey walked beside her and trustingly put his small hand in hers. "Who's he?" he said, pointing.

"My father."

"Does he know Des, too?"

"He knew Des a long time ago," she said, narrowing her gaze on the man who'd orchestrated her hurt.

"When he was a kid like me?"

"Not quite that long ago," she clarified.

Trey studied Carter Richmond. "Did you know Des kissed Miss Molly?"

"No. When did this happen?" Carter asked, frowning.

Trey was on a roll. "When my mom had her car crash and was in the hopspittle. I stayed with Miss Molly and Des came over to help me build stuff. I couldn't sleep and then I saw him kissin' her."

Molly's cheeks burned. She'd had no idea the child remembered seeing their kiss. "Look, Dad—"

"So the rumors circulating all over town are true. The two of you are engaged."

"About that—"

The door opened and Trey's mom hurried inside. The pretty blonde smiled apologetically. "Hi, Miss Molly. Sorry I'm late. Traffic."

"Mommy!" The little boy grabbed her jeans-clad leg.

"Hi, baby." She bent and hugged him. "Are you ready to go home?"

He nodded. "Can we have chicken nuggets and French fries for dinner?"

"If you have some fruit and a veggie, too."

"Deal." He looked up. "Bye, Miss Molly."

"See you tomorrow, sweetie." She waved to mother and son just before the door closed.

Molly couldn't help thinking the child was better off with a loving mother than a manipulative bastard of a father. Like hers. Or Des's. At least Des's father had an excuse. Alcoholism was an illness he'd been too weak to overcome. Her own father was simply shallow and self-absorbed. It was time—way past time—to rewrite another part of her history.

"Dad, I want to talk to you about Des."

"I always liked his drive and ambition."

"You used those qualities to get what you wanted," she said.

"I beg your pardon?"

"As well you should. I know about the deal you made with Des to pay attention to me."

Instead of shock or surprise, he simply looked bored. "There was a secrecy clause in that agreement."

"Bummer," she said. It hit her that he didn't even care enough to question how she'd found out.

"That would explain your coolness toward me."

"I'm surprised you noticed." Although clearly his focus was on how the discovery impacted him, not on the devastation she had felt.

"In my defense, I'd like to say that I had your best interests at heart. And my wife approved."

Molly had said as much to Des. "Ah, yes. Gorgeous Gabrielle."

"Yes," he said, smiling. "She is lovely."

"On the ouside. She treated me like a redheaded stepchild."

"You are her redheaded stepchild."

"The problem is, *you* treated me that way, too." Molly huffed out a breath. It was interesting how the grievances stacked up inside her kept popping out. It was exhilarating and liberating. "Instead of protecting me—defending me—the way a father should, you jumped on her bandwagon because you believed I wasn't good enough just the way I was. Fathers should stand up for their daughters. And you didn't stand up for me." Someone like Carter Richmond wasn't deserving of her deference. "I love you, Dad, because you're my father. But I don't like you. And I don't respect you because you've done nothing to earn it. In fact, just the opposite."

She wasn't Carter Richmond's doormat any longer because she knew him for what he was. Only someone she held in high esteem had the power to hurt her.

"I suppose I can understand why you feel this way," he conceded reluctantly. "But as far as standing up for yourself—you don't need me or anyone else. You've apparently figured out how to do it on your own."

Once, the spark of admiration in his eyes would have meant the world to her. Now—not so much. If not for Des, she probably wouldn't have confronted her father. Des had shown her that standing up to life was far better than letting it walk all over her.

The door opened again and Molly held her breath,

anticipating the hard-hat hunk she'd just been thinking about. Instead of Des, Judy Abbott walked inside.

"Hi, Molly."

"Judy."

The woman eyed Carter and clearly approved of what she saw. "Who's the Dennis Farina look-alike?"

"My father. Carter Richmond. Dad, this is Judy Abbott—someone Des knew in New York."

They shook hands and exchanged the appropriate greeting before Judy asked, "Is Des here?"

Molly glanced around, then gave her a "duh" look. "A man that size is pretty hard to hide."

"Simmer down, darling. You win. I give up. I'm going back to New York."

"You are?"

"Why were you here?" Carter asked, clearly confused.

"I didn't just know Des. We were engaged."

"There's a lot of that going around." He glanced at Molly. "Were?"

"I broke it off when he announced his intention to come back to his hometown and work in construction," Judy said.

"I see," he said, eyes narrowing. "But that doesn't explain what you're doing here."

"I wanted to see if I could rekindle the spark." She shot Molly a spiteful look. "But it's not going to happen. Someone else has engaged him."

"Des isn't here," Molly said quickly. "Why don't you look at his office?"

"Already been there and he wasn't in. I'm on my way to the airport for the flight home and wanted to tell him goodbye. And good luck."

"I'll pass that along." Happiness danced through Molly and she struggled not to grin like a loon.

"Okay. Thanks. Gotta run." Judy reached the door, then looked back. "He's a keeper," she said before leaving.

"She's quite an attractive young woman," her father said, staring at the spot where the other woman had been moments before.

"If you like skin and bones," Molly muttered.

Her father looked at his watch. "As fascinating as this is, Molly, I didn't stop by to air our dirty laundry."

"Thanks for the newsflash," she said, relishing this new sarcastic streak of hers. "So why *did* you stop by?"

"I'm monitoring the work O'Donnell Construction is doing on your expansion."

"Professional curiosity?"

"Some," he admitted. "I always wondered if my investment in Des's future paid off. Then he came back to town to run his family's business and I wanted to see what he could do with that drive and ambition."

"You saw for yourself the outstanding quality of workmanship. Not only that, the project is coming in ahead of schedule and under budget."

"And you know this how?"

"The preschool director announced it at the staff meeting."

Carter nodded as he idly glanced toward the windows looking out on the expansion. "So it would seem that he's on his way to achieving the goal that brought him back to Charity City."

"On his way?" Odd way to phrase it. "He came back to build things with his own two hands, the way his grandfather taught him, and he's doing just that."

"It's more than that, Molly. O'Donnell Construction is about to go under. The word is that Des came back to keep that from happening. In essence, to save his company."

A shiver of unease rippled through her. Des hadn't mentioned recent business problems. He'd only said how tough things were when he was in high school. She'd assumed the company was doing all right now.

Her father slid his hands in his pockets. "For years O'Donnell's has been struggling. Not many in the business are willing to take a chance on them."

"That's not Des's fault," she said defensively. "He's saddled with the reputation his father's carelessness earned the company. All Des needs is time and someone to give him a chance to turn things around."

"The building contract with Richmond Homes would do that." He held her gaze. "We're planning a new development project and Des put in a bid. I've narrowed down the field and O'Donnell is one of the two remaining candidates."

"Does Des know?" She dreaded hearing the answer.

Carter nodded. "For a while now."

Molly's stomach knotted and turned over. After

several minutes of small talk she didn't really hear, her father left.

So much for Des not being able to hurt her anymore. So much for not being fooled a second time. It was officially déjà vu all over again.

Des was using her to get something he wanted from her father.

Chapter Eleven

Des closed his cell phone as he was pulling into the apartment complex. He parked and let out a whoop of triumph. "Hot *damn!*"

All the worry and work and stress had been worth the blood, sweat and fears. It felt as if things were finally falling into place—professionally and personally. All he could think about was telling Molly the good news and seeing her eyes light up like fireworks on New Year's Eve. Wasn't it convenient that they lived in the same complex? Not as convenient as living under the same roof, sleeping in the same bed and being able to touch her and hold her all night.

"Where'd that come from?" he muttered to himself.

Might have something to do with that hot kiss they'd

shared in the parking lot outside her gym. He swore he'd felt the earth move. For her, too. The feelings he had for her were different from anything he'd ever known. But he couldn't think about that now. He had to tell Molly the good news and somehow he'd wound up at her place where he took the steps two at a time.

He knocked on her door and felt as if he'd explode if she wasn't home. He glanced at the window and saw that the lights were on. She must be home. Then he heard footsteps just on the other side of the door and knew she was checking through the peephole. If they lived together, security precautions wouldn't be quite as important because he'd be there to take care of her.

Again the thoughts. Was his subconscious trying to get a message through?

What was taking her so long to answer? He was sure he'd heard footsteps and now he was starting to worry. He knocked again. "Molly? It's me. Des. I have to talk to you."

Still she didn't open the door and he sensed that she was trying to decide whether or not she would. What was going on? When he'd kissed her, he knew she'd felt it clear down to her toes. He would bet everything he had or ever hoped to have that things between them were good and going to get better.

He lifted his hand to knock again when the door opened. "Hey. I was about to huff and puff and blow your house down."

"What do you want?"

He looked closer. Speaking of puff—her eyes were

swollen. And red, as if she'd been crying. In her black sweatpants and white T-shirt with her red hair pulled into a ponytail on top of her head, she was hands-down the sexiest woman he'd ever laid eyes on. And if she'd tell him who'd made her cry, he'd go beat them up.

"What's wrong?" he asked, stepping inside without waiting for an invitation.

"Allergies," she said, sniffling. "Why are you here?"

Allergies, his backside, but one look at her face told him not to push. "I had a talk with your father."

"There's a lot of that going around."

"What?"

"My father came by the school earlier."

He closed the door since she didn't seem inclined to, and the implication that he wasn't welcome to stay bothered him.

"What did he say?" If the old bastard had hurt her, Des would take him apart.

"Actually I did most of the talking." She pulled at the used tissue in her hands.

They still stood by the door and it was on the tip of his tongue to ask if he could sit down, but, based on past experience with her looking the way she looked, he figured he'd get a no. He'd been climbing the slippery mountain of Molly's affections and nearly made it to the top, but somehow he'd slid back down. Lower than before. And he wasn't sure why—or, more important, why it mattered so much. But he was pretty sure it had something to do with her father.

He folded his arms over his chest. "Tell me what happened."

"Actually we talked about you."

"Me?"

"He said he'd always wondered what happened to you because your drive and ambition impressed him."

"Does he know you know about—" he hated even saying it "—about the deal I made with him?"

She nodded. "He didn't seem overly concerned that I'd found out."

"So you told him off?" Her surprised look made him add, "You said you did most of the talking."

"Oh. Yes. I told him exactly what I thought about what he did. That fathers are supposed to protect their kids, not give other kids ammo for their teasing and taunting."

"How did he take that?" Des asked.

"As usual, he made it all about him. But I still felt better."

The strain on her face and evidence of tears didn't support that statement. "Don't take this the wrong way, but you don't look better. What's going on?"

"That's what I'd like to know." She balled the tissue in her fist. "Why didn't you tell me O'Donnell Construction was in serious financial trouble? All you said was that you came back to run the family business after your father died."

"That's true. I came back for all the reasons I told you. And because I couldn't stand by and do nothing while the company my grandfather started went down the tubes."

"But you neglected to mention how bad things really are."

He ran his fingers through his hair, wondering why his business was suddenly an issue. "I told you how bad it was when I was in high school and that my father's drinking problem didn't get any better. It finally killed him." He looked away, not wanting to see the pity in her eyes again.

"You left a lot more out," she accused.

He met her disapproving gaze. "It's not a good idea to put negative details out for public consumption when trying to rebuild a company. Present a solid front and all that. Or you don't inspire confidence in prospective clients."

"So you think I'd have blabbed?"

"No. I don't know. I guess I didn't think it through." Mostly because he'd been thinking about the way she made him laugh and kept him on his toes as easily as she turned him on. "Why are you making such a big deal out of this?"

Shaking her head, she sighed and looked away for a moment. "Why did you come over here, Des?"

When he'd seen how upset she was, everything else had gone out of his head. "I had some good news today."

"My father awarded you the Richmond Homes development project." It wasn't a question.

Now it was his turn to be surprised and it must have

shown because she said, "He told me today that he'd narrowed the slate to two and you said you just talked with my father."

He nodded. "He just called. I couldn't wait to tell you. I've invested a lot of time and money into the business and this will turn the corner for us."

"So everything you've done has been about the company?"

It crossed his mind that she wasn't talking about business, but he blundered ahead. "It's the break I've been hoping for."

"Not such a break," she said, her tone cold and hurt.

"What do you mean?"

"It seems like when you stack the deck in your favor, calling it a 'break' is just wrong."

"If you call working twelve- to fourteen-hour days and sweating over the smallest details stacking the deck, then I plead guilty."

"You're guilty, but it's not about working. It's about you and my father and deals—at my expense. Again."

He stared at her, feeling as if she'd slugged him in the gut. "What are you saying?"

"You came back to town and paid attention to me so my father would give you the building contract to salvage your business."

"That's not true," he said angrily. "You bought me at the auction. Remember?"

"That was about settling high-school scores," she defended.

"Apparently they're not settled if you think I'd use you like that."

"I don't think it. I know. Everyone knows. Mike implied it at the reunion. You used me and it paid off."

"You're wrong, Molly."

"The timing of your good news is a little suspect, though," she continued, as if he hadn't spoken. "I tell my father off and he calls to give you what you want. Could it be that he's trying to get back in my good graces by buying you for me again?"

"This is crazy," Des said, anger and frustration coiling together inside him. The combination wasn't especially good for logical thinking.

"Oh?"

"There's no deal with your father. I got the contract because my company is best for the job and I've got the business and building expertise to produce a quality product on time and within budget."

"Keep telling yourself that."

"I can do this, Molly," he said, taking a step toward her. Her look stopped him. "When I do, it will cement my reputation and undo all the damage my father did for so many years. I wish he was here—and my grandfather—to see the company getting back on track."

For a split second, a softness stole into her eyes, then she shook her head and stood a little straighter. "That's really touching. I suppose making it all about family honor will help you sleep nights."

"For God's sake, Molly, you're not thinking clearly."

"On the contrary," she said, green eyes flashing, "for the first time in my life I *am* thinking clearly. And here's what I'm thinking. The old Molly would have been grateful for any crumbs of affection you tossed her way. But the new-and-improved Molly doesn't need you."

"You've got to listen to me—"

"Not again. Not anymore. Apparently it's my day for growing a spine. I told my father off and now it's your turn. I can't afford to believe you ever again." She brushed past him and opened the door. "Now, please leave."

He didn't budge. "You don't mean that."

"I do. I mean it just as much as I mean I'll get over loving you."

"You love me?"

"As if you didn't know." She laughed bitterly. "If I didn't, you couldn't have used me again, let alone with such spectacular success. I can't believe anything you say or do, yet I care. How dumb am I? Apparently dumb enough to feel that way about men who don't deserve it. But I'm turning over a new leaf. I'll get over it. Now, please go."

The only reason he did as she asked was because her bombshell had stunned him. As soon as she slammed the door behind him, he knew it had been a mistake to move. She'd never let him back in.

And now that he was out, he realized how very important it was that he somehow change her mind.

* * *

The corporate offices of Richmond Homes were housed in their very own building on the corner of Benevolent Boulevard and Welfare Way across from Philanthropy Plaza in the heart of Charity City. At ten stories, it was probably the most imposing structure in town, all red brick and tall windows. Standing on the street, Des looked up and wished he didn't need the contract with Carter Richmond.

Angry, frustrated and tired, Des marched inside, ready to take his bad mood out on the devil himself if Satan was dumb enough to get in his way. When the elevator arrived in the lobby, he stepped inside and pushed the up button. He got out on the top floor and looked around, not surprised Carter Richmond's pretentious domain was all silver and glass, symbolic of the smoke, mirrors and manipulation so much a part of the man.

After giving his name to the receptionist, he was immediately admitted entrance to the inner sanctum. When the heavy door opened, Carter Richmond was waiting for him.

"Des, my boy, welcome to the Richmond family." The older man looked at him more closely. "Good Lord, you look like hell."

"Thank you. I feel like hell." A direct result of not sleeping.

"Ah." Richmond nodded his approval. "Out celebrating the new contract."

"No."

He'd been too busy kicking himself for his stupidity. Molly had told him she loved him. But that didn't mean he could ever have it. Not after the mess he'd made of everything.

"Why did you give me the contract?"

Carter looked at him, surprised. Apparently the old man had expected major ass-kissing. That wasn't going to happen.

"Let's sit down," Carter said, indicating the two leather-and-chrome chairs in front of his glass-and-chrome desk.

Des looked around the large corner office that offered two different city views. Bookcases, art, sculptures and glass were scattered around, all modern and soulless. None of it was warm. This room held no hint that this cold, cruel, callous bastard had provided the DNA for the vibrant, tenderhearted redhead he'd fathered.

Richmond sat down behind his desk. "Des, have a seat."

"I'll stand." Chalk one up for Molly.

"Suit yourself." The older man's gaze narrowed. "Now, what's the problem?"

"Why did you award the housing contract to O'Donnell Construction?" he asked again.

"I had my reasons."

So the man wanted to play twenty questions. Des could do that. "I'm asking for those reasons."

"All right." Carter nodded, his scrutiny obviously

picking up on Des's determination to get the answers he was after. "Obviously your bid was competitive. You're hungry, which is a damn good guarantee of giving me an outstanding job. I liked what I saw at the preschool expansion. Company owner hands-on and on-site. Good workmanship."

"But Matthews is all of that and they've had a consistently better reputation over the years. Why did you give it to me?"

"I like you, Des. You're young, enthusiastic, ambitious and driven."

There it was again. Ambition and drive biting him in the backside. He put his palms down on the glass desk leaving two full sets of fingerprints. Leaning forward, he said, "Let's get something straight. I'm no longer a teenage kid desperate for a way out."

Richmond leaned back in his chair and rested his elbows on the arms. "I'm aware of that."

"And if you think you can use my company's financial situation to control me and get your own way, think again."

"The thought never crossed my mind."

Des knew that was a lie. "So I got the contract on my own?" he asked, straightening.

"Of course."

"It had nothing to do with Molly?"

Richmond picked up a gold pen and twisted it open, then closed. "Why do you ask?"

"Because you're you. And your track record speaks

for itself. You're not above using interference and manipulation to get what you want."

Ice-blue eyes narrowed. "And what would that be?"

"Your daughter's forgiveness." Des folded his arms over his chest. "She told me about standing up to you after all these years."

Richmond nodded, but the chink in his confidence was evident. "Most impressive."

"So Molly had something to do with your decision?"

"I admit my daughter's feelings tipped the scale in your favor."

"Define *feelings*."

"She's in love with you."

"How do you know?" Had she told the old man?

"I knew it when she vehemently defended O'Donnell Construction and urged me to give you an opportunity to improve the company's tarnished reputation."

That was Molly. Wearing her heart on her sleeve.

"Was that before or after you mentioned that I'd come home to save my grandfather's company?"

"I really don't recall. And I don't see what difference it makes."

All the difference in the world. But this time, Richmond didn't deserve to be read the riot act. Des was taking out his frustration because he was mad at himself. He should have been the one to tell Molly. But she was just beginning to trust him again and he'd been afraid she'd go back to the bad place where she didn't. *Fool me once, shame on you. Fool me twice, shame on me.* If she'd known he needed something from her father, no way would she have let him close a second time.

Des let out a long breath. "The difference is that she wants nothing to do with me now that she knows. She thinks I'm using her for a stepping stone to success."

"I'm sorry to hear that."

Yeah, he looked real sorry. "She believes that now I have what I want, I'll drop her like a hot rock."

She was definitely hot, Des thought. But there was nothing hard about her. Especially her soft, marshmallow heart, which she'd managed to harden on his account. She was good and kind. Loyal and funny and smart. The truth hit him like a two-by-four in a twister.

He was in love with Molly. He looked at Carter Richmond and knew what he had to do to try to win back her love.

Chapter Twelve

Being in love with Des O'Donnell was bad enough, Molly thought, but she'd made matters worse by not keeping the information to herself.

"Big blabbermouth," she muttered, as she set a bag of groceries on the island in her kitchen.

It had been a long day and she'd been tired when she woke up. Actually, waking would require going to sleep first and she hadn't. At least not much. Thoughts of Des, memories of his mouth on hers, being in his arms, feeling cherished, made it almost impossible to rest. When she'd managed it, flashes of his serial duplicity snapped her awake again. She'd been so certain that this time he was interested in her, but this time he'd been pretending only to get the contract from her father that would save O'Donnell Construction.

If he'd told her up front…if he'd revealed that he was in the running for the Richmond Homes contract… What? She'd never know if she'd have cut him some slack because he hadn't confided in her.

If there was a silver lining, it was that this time he'd suffer public humiliation. She would put out the word that she broke off her engagement to Des because she realized she didn't love him. Tears welled in her eyes at the lie. If only it were true.

The phone rang, startling her and she sniffed as she checked the caller ID to make certain it wasn't Des. She didn't want to talk to him. But the readout said Private which didn't help her much. She let the call go to her answering machine and, when she heard her father's voice, she picked up.

"Hello, Dad." Apparently she was a magnet for manipulative males. Lucky her. She'd picked up the call because old habits died hard. Some old habits, like Des, refused to die. But Carter Richmond she could handle now. "I don't have anything to say to you."

"Then just listen. You have to convince your boyfriend"

"I don't have a boyfriend."

"Are you telling me you're not in love with Des O'Donnell?"

"I'm not telling you anything except that I have no boyfriend."

"Ah. That's right. You've itemized your grievances

and declared your independence. But whether you like it or not, you're still my daughter."

"What do you want, Dad?"

"Tell Des he's a fool."

"If I were speaking to him, it would be my pleasure. But why would I be telling him that?"

"Because he turned down my offer."

Stunned didn't come close to describing what Molly felt. She sank onto the sofa. Des didn't take the development contract? Was this some kind of joke? Worse, was it a conspiracy between Des and her father? It wouldn't be the first time.

"Molly?" he barked. "Are you there? Did you hear what I said?"

"Yes." She shook her head to clear it. "I heard you."

"What is that tone in your voice?"

"It's called once burned, twice shy. I'm not sure what kind of game you're playing, but this time you can count me out."

"This isn't a game, Molly. That idiot O'Donnell flatly refused to honor our verbal agreement."

"Why would he do that?"

"Because he's in love with you."

If Molly hadn't already been sitting, her legs wouldn't have held her upright. For a man who knew so little about love, her father was throwing the word around like a Frisbee. Why should she listen to him? The man wouldn't know love if it zapped him with a power drill.

"Now I know you're after something," she said.

"I never said I wasn't. You talk to him and convince him to take my offer. The success of his business depends on it."

"Goodbye, Dad."

She hit the phone's off button before he could say more. She didn't want to be more confused than she already was. If her dad was telling the truth, why in the world had Des turned down the deal that would bail out his company? She couldn't afford to believe his decision had anything to do with her. Bad enough to have her heart broken, even worse to be made a fool of in the process.

A knock on her door startled her for the second time in five minutes. What was this? Communication central? She checked through the peephole, then gasped and jumped back. Des! Double whammy. She'd like to know which of the fates she'd offended, so she could take it back and stop this retribution.

Des knocked again, louder this time. "Molly, I need to talk to you."

"No."

"I won't take no for an answer."

"Then how about this answer—I don't want to talk to you."

"Unacceptable. I understand how you feel, but I'm not leaving until you hear me out."

She couldn't do this; she couldn't bear it. Why couldn't he just leave her alone and give her time and space to get over him? That was when she realized all the time and space on the planet wouldn't be enough to get over him. It was never going to happen. Of course, that didn't mean she had to let him into her space—to see him, smell his wonderful masculine scent, feel his warmth and watch helplessly as her resolve melted.

"Okay," she shouted through the door. "You've got two minutes."

"Open the door. I'm not going to say this loud enough for downtown Charity City to hear."

Now what? If they kept shouting at each other, the neighbors would hear. Their peace would be disturbed. Someone might call the police. Nervously, she chewed on her lip, trying to decide which was the lesser of two evils.

"Molly?" He pounded on the door.

"Stop shouting." She turned the dead bolt and opened the door. His eyes were bloodshot and stubble covered his jaw. Deep lines carved into his face beside his nose and mouth. "You look terrible."

Just like she felt. Tired. Desperate. Frustrated. Angry. And very, very sad.

"You have to listen to me," he said, entering her apartment and coming to a stop in her living room.

"Okay. But I have a question first. Did you turn down my father's offer?"

"Yes." He turned and blinked. "How did you know?"

"I just got off the phone with him." She remained standing just inside the door, staring at him. "Why?"

"Because of you."

"Me?"

He nodded. "If I'd signed on the dotted line, you'd never have believed I didn't use you to get it." Despair mixed with sincerity in his voice.

"But what about the business? It's why you came back. Your grandfather started it. What if you lose it? It could happen."

"It could," he agreed. "It's possible. But there's something even more important to me."

"What?" she asked, holding her breath.

"You." Blue eyes searched hers—seeking, hoping, expectant.

The sincerity in his expression, the passion in his voice, what he'd given up: all of that convinced Molly that Des was telling the truth.

"Oh, my." A lump of emotion thickened in her throat.

His long legs chewed up the distance between them. He took her hands in his and held on tight. "I'm so sorry I hurt you."

"It's all right."

"No. I'd rather lose everything I have than see the pain in your eyes."

"I don't want you to lose anything. Take the contract."

He shook his head. "I realized I don't want to work for Carter Richmond. No one knows better than me what a game-player he is, and I don't want any part of that. I don't want him calling the shots for me, but especially not for you. I'll figure out another way."

"There's my trust fund. I could invest in the business."

A tender look softened the fierce expression on his face. "Nothing has ever touched me more." He brought her hand to his lips and kissed her knuckles. "But I couldn't take your money."

"But you needed my father's contract."

"I've got other irons in the fire. This would just be the fastest, smartest way to reach my goal and preserve operating capital. But if I took the deal and lost you, it would be the dumbest thing I ever did."

"That reminds me," she said, "my father said to tell you you're a fool. And I believe he called you, and I quote, 'that idiot O'Donnell.'"

"Remind me to thank him."

"What for?"

"For you. Thanks to you, I realized that business accomplishments aren't the measure of a man." He squeezed her hands. "Just look at your father."

"Good point."

"Can we sit down?" he asked.

She nodded. They sat side by side on the sofa, thighs brushing, generating heat and sparks and hope.

Des leaned forward, resting his elbows on his knees and linking his fingers. "Success is finding satisfaction in the work you do, not in how much it pays. You taught me that."

"Me?"

"Yes, you." He smiled. "I came back because I didn't like what I was doing in New York. More important, I saw you loving what you do every day and not getting rich. But you're happy."

"I love my kids," she said simply.

"And they love you. You're a very good teacher, Miss Molly. I've learned a lot from you."

"Really?"

He nodded. "You taught me that it's not the size of your bank account that matters, but the size of your heart. And yours is as big as Texas."

"Oh, Des—"

"After Judy, I didn't think a woman could love me for me. But everything about you said you were different. When you said you'd follow me anywhere, that scared me. So I put up barriers, telling myself you were your father's daughter. And likely into control and appearances, too. If I believed what my instincts told me, I'd have to put my feelings on the line and take a risk."

"And how do you feel now?"

He grinned. "My instincts were right on the money. I knew it that very first day in the classroom, *Polly* Preston."

"Those rhyming names." She laughed.

"You had paint on your hands and the welfare of your kids on your mind."

"It's the best job I ever had and everything I've ever wanted to do."

"You believed in your dream and because of your example, I've decided to follow mine."

Oh, God. What did that mean? Was he trying to let

her down easy? She took a deep breath and said, "Whatever you do I hope you'll be happy."

"That depends on you." He looked into her eyes. "You're my dream, Molly. I love you. Only you. You make me happy."

"You don't know—"

He held up his hand. "I know you've got doubts, but from this day on, I swear I'll never give you reason to question my love. I'll work for your trust. I'll be—"

She touched her fingers to his mouth, stopping the flow of words. "I have no doubts. You don't know how much I love you."

He let out a long, shuddering breath, then pulled her onto his lap and held her against him with fierce possessiveness. His eyes brimmed with tender emotion before he lowered his mouth to hers and kissed the living daylights out of her.

"I can't believe I got so lucky," he said when they came up for air.

She cupped his cheek in her palm, loving the roughness of his stubble that made her palm tingle. "There's a lot of that going around. I loved you when I was a girl and I never stopped. I guess I'll always love you."

"Then I guess you'll just have to put me out of my misery and make me the happiest man in the world. Marry me, Molly."

"Just try and stop me."

Epilogue

Molly carefully picked her way over rocks, nails, discarded wallboard and pieces of wood at one of the construction sites where her husband was supervising a project.

Husband.

It had been three months and the reality of marrying Des was still sinking in. But wrapped in each other's arms every night was tangible proof of their love and deep commitment.

Des looked up from the building plans he was studying and grinned. "Hey, wife. This is an unexpected pleasant surprise."

"Hi." She tapped her lip as she gave him the once-over.

"What?" he asked, frowning.

"I was just thinking how very hunklike you look in your hard hat."

"You like it?" he asked, shifting it to a rakish angle. "What do I get if I model it for you when we're alone later?"

"Anything you want."

"I like the sound of that." He slid her a suggestive look, then took her in his arms and kissed her until her breath grew ragged. When he pulled away, he said, "To what do I owe the pleasure of this visit?"

His voice was husky and the word *pleasure* had sent tingles shimmying up and down her spine. With an effort, she pulled herself together. "I've got some good news and some bad. Which do you want first?"

His brow puckered. "Bad."

"My father called again. The company he put in charge of his newest development isn't performing to his expectations. He said the least his son-in-law could do is bail him out."

"Fat chance." Des laughed. "The preschool project brought in a lot of word-of-mouth customers. My good reputation is growing, and I've got about all the business I can handle until the expansion plans for O'Donnell Construction are implemented. Why should I put all that on the line for an old schemer like your father?"

"That's what I told him. Except for the schemer part."

"You're way too nice, Mrs. O'Donnell." He bent and kissed the tip of her nose. "So what's the good news?"

"I hope you'll think it's good," she said, twisting her fingers together. "This is a little sooner than we planned. I'm not sure we—"

"Molly?"

"I'm pregnant," she said, then held her breath.

"Pregnant? As in having-a-baby pregnant?"

"Yes."

"Are you all right?"

"Yes. He's fine, too."

"He?"

"I've got a feeling."

For several moments his face was frozen with shock and surprise. Then he let out a whoop and pulled her into his arms, lifting her off her feet to swing her around.

Just as suddenly, he set her down again, concern etched on his handsome features. He touched her face, her arms, and checked her over from head to toe. "Did I hurt you? The baby? Does this mean I'm a bad father already?"

"Not even close." Her joy spilled over as she laughed and cried at the same time. "Between the two of us we've experienced some of the paternal potholes." Then she turned serious as she met his clear blue gaze. "I believe we've learned from our fathers' mistakes. Whatever we do wrong will be all on our own."

He put his hand on her still-flat belly. "What an awesome responsibility."

"Yeah." She put her hand over his. "And speaking of

responsibility, I have to get back to school. It's my lunch break. I just couldn't wait until tonight to tell you."

"I'll walk you back to the car."

They started off hand in hand, but when she stumbled a little on a rock, Des swore and scooped her into his arms.

She squealed, then rested her hand on his broad shoulder. "For Pete's sake, Des, I'm not a delicate flower. Pregnancy is the most normal thing in the world."

"Not to me. You're pregnant with our baby. I'm not taking any chances, Mrs. O'Donnell."

Molly sighed and snuggled into his arms. She liked the sound of that. Who'd have guessed the girl once voted least likely to attract a man now had the guy she'd always wanted and a baby on the way? In her wildest dreams she'd never thought she could be this happy.

The past was past. The future had never looked brighter. And the present... She kissed her hard-hat hunk on the cheek and figured he was a present she would unwrap later—when they were home alone.

* * * * *

Don't miss the conclusion to BUY-A-GUY *with*
SOMETHING'S GOTTA GIVE by Teresa Southwick
Silhouette Romance #1814
Available May 2006!